twenty

twenty

Debra Landwehr Engle

KENSINGTON BOOKS
www.kensingtonbooks.com

KENSINGTON BOOKS are published by

Kensington Publishing Corp.
119 West 40th Street
New York, NY 10018

All Kensington titles, imprints, and distributed lines are available at special quantity discounts for bulk purchases for sales promotion, premiums, fund-raising, educational, or institutional use.

Special book excerpts or customized printings can also be created to fit specific needs. For details, write or phone the office of the Kensington Sales Manager: Kensington Publishing Corp., 119 West 40th Street, New York, NY 10018. Attn. Sales Department. Phone: 1-800-221-2647.

Kensington and the K logo Reg. U.S. Pat. & TM Off.

ISBN-13: 978-1-4967-2358-1 (ebook)
ISBN-10: 1-4967-2358-9 (ebook)
Kensington Electronic Edition: February 2020

ISBN-13: 978-1-4967-2357-4
ISBN-10: 1-4967-2357-0
First Kensington Trade Paperback Printing: February 2020

10 9 8 7 6 5 4 3 2 1

Printed in the United States of America

To all who struggle, there is light ahead

DAY ONE

Early this morning, long before the sun came up, I took the pill bottle out of the freezer, looked at the green drops of gelatin that shimmered like pearls, and stirred them into my raspberry yogurt. I watched them lose their color and melt down until they disappeared, the way marshmallows do when I make ambrosia.

It was 3:27 a.m. I checked the time on Daddy's mantel clock, and I sent myself an e-mail on my phone to mark the moment. I was 80 percent certain taking the pearls was the right thing to do. It surprises me that I'd take such a step without knowing for sure. But how *could* I know?

Maybe the pearls lost their potency long ago. Maybe they were a hoax all along. Maybe they won't work the way Dr. Edelman told me on the day when it sleeted and my umbrella turned inside out.

I licked the yogurt off my spoon and settled back into my chair, as though I'd just finished some of Mama's pork chops, and stared out the kitchen window at the darkness, letting myself sink into the quiet. I didn't feel any different. Of course, I didn't know what to expect. Would my toes start to tingle? Would my lips turn blue? Would I suddenly clutch my chest and fall to the floor? Not likely. From what Dr. Edelman said, I may feel better than I've felt my whole life. Wouldn't that be something? Wouldn't that be the way to go?

I propped my feet up on the red chair, knowing the first light of dawn would arrive in just a couple of hours, bringing relentless heat with it. Every day for weeks, there has been nothing but sun. It glares through the windows and lights up the room, making it a little too easy to see a thin layer of dust on Mama's angel collection. It glances off the toaster and the stainless steel canisters.

In a normal Iowa summer, thunderstorms and tornadoes crop up like weeds. How many years would we have given anything for such a string of preposterously bright days? But this summer we've had nothing but outrageous heat and an endlessly cloudless sky. Every day I step out the screen door to check on the gardens, and every day I see that my herbs are browner around the edges. The leaves of my black-eyed Susans are sagging, and the grass looks like hay, snapping when I drag the hose across the yard to keep everything barely alive.

Day before yesterday, the temperature hit 106 degrees at four in the afternoon. While I watered the flowers for the fourth time that day, I listened to the spray drumming against the leaves of the coneflowers and hostas, and I had a familiar feeling. The plants weren't responding anymore. They looked parched and exhausted, as if they'd given up. No matter what I do, I can't revive them.

"Some years it's like this," I said to them. I looked around the yard at each one of them, just like when I volunteered in Rose's class and tried to make eye contact with every student. "Some years it's too much rain, other years it's too little. I wish I could give you everything you need, but it's out of my hands."

I wrapped the hose around its holder on the side of the

house, left my dusty garden shoes at the kitchen door, and came inside to wash my face with cool water. Then I stretched out in bed, not even bothering to turn down Mama's quilt, and slept until the sun came up yesterday morning.

I come from a long line of flowers. Mama's name was Lillian, and her mother was Camellia, a rather exotic name for a woman on the prairie. Along with naming me Marguerite after her favorite daisy, Mama gave me three things: Red hair that hasn't faded. A love of nature. And a belief that somewhere between heaven and earth there is magic.

I still remember when I was five years old and we were out in the backyard. Mama hung Daddy's T-shirts on the clothesline, and Holly played in the playhouse that Daddy built for us. He'd painted it white with green shutters, just like the house in our favorite Little Golden Book.

I helped Mama, handing her the heavy, damp shirts from the laundry basket. Suddenly she stopped, holding a clothespin in midair, and said to me, "They're here, Meg. Can you feel them all around you?"

I was wearing my favorite blue gingham pinafore with the kitten appliqué and a white bow in my hair because I'd just gotten off the bus, home from kindergarten. I remember nodding my head and closing my eyes. I felt a brush of air against my cheek and ankles, then a beam of light warming the right side of my face. But I could also see and smell them, something that had never happened before. They were like swirls of perfumed air wrapping themselves around me.

"I *see* them," I said. I remember the startled look on Mama's face.

"What do they look like?" she asked me.

"They're pink and yellow and blue and green," I said.

I felt peaceful. Whatever I saw felt familiar to me, like a memory.

"They're tickling me," I said, and Mama laughed, that tinkly chime of a laugh she had before everything changed.

"Don't ever forget them," Mama said. "They're always with you."

I nodded my head, then put my hands in the air and turned in a circle. "I'll remember," I said. I know Mama hoped I would.

I felt those swirls and breaths and tickles, wearing them like a shawl two months later when, on a blustery November day, we buried Daddy after the train wreck. Mama wore a pillbox hat like the President's wife and a tailored black suit with a black wool coat that had a fur collar. Holly was too young to remember, but I never forgot it. How dreary the day felt, how I'd never seen Mama cry like that, how gray and brown and black everything seemed.

Then, in the middle of the service by that awful hole in the ground, when the minister recited the 23rd Psalm, I saw the bright colors swirling and dancing in front of me. I reached out to touch them and smiled, and Mama didn't try to stop me because she knew what I was seeing and wished she could see them, too.

By the time I was seven, though, I no longer saw the colors or felt the whispers on my cheek. I felt lonelier somehow, but I didn't know why, so I busied myself teaching Holly how to dress Barbie in her emerald-green ball gown with the taffeta skirt, and how to brush her blond hair so it would shine when Ken picked her up for their date.

"How handsome you look," I said to Ken one day, using my best high-pitched Barbie voice. "You'll make a very good dad."

Not until years later, when Joe and I had Rose, did I realize what a big hole Daddy's death left in our lives.

* * *

Mama died five years ago today. Holly called before I left for work, which was early in Seattle.

"Hey, sis," she said. "Just thought I'd catch you before you left for the day." It was good to hear her voice, but I knew she was calling to check on me, and I felt tears come immediately. I didn't know I was that fragile.

"Good timing," I said, trying to sound casual. "I'm just finishing my coffee. How are you doing this morning?"

"Not bad," she said. "The kids are still in bed. They don't go back to school for a couple of weeks, so they're sleeping in while they can. And Phil went out for an early run. I was just getting myself some breakfast and thought I'd say hi. I know this day is hard for you."

"For you, too." I gazed out the window at the shed and the hills behind the house and tried to focus on the present.

"Sure, but my life didn't change like yours did when Mama died. I don't know what she'd have done without you."

"Yeah, I do miss her," I said, clenching the edge of the kitchen counter and willing myself not to cry. Five years. When would I ever move on?

"I'm sure you do," Holly said. "She was something, wasn't she?"

I paused, swallowed, and tried to keep my voice from breaking. Holly wouldn't have minded, but I'm tired of being pitiful. "No question," I said, slipping on my shoes to distract myself. "I don't know how she kept everything going after Daddy died. She never let on how much she struggled. After all that courage, she deserved a better final few years."

"I don't know," Holly said. "You made those years the best they could be. I hope you know how much I appreciate that, Meg. You gave up a lot for her."

I paced the kitchen, opened the refrigerator, sat down at the table, and stood up again—anything to keep my voice from cracking on the phone. "We needed each other," I said. "I think she helped me more than I helped her." I could feel myself starting to break.

"Anyway," I said, "I'd better get going. I need to help Nancy open the shop for the day."

"Sure," Holly said. "Say, if you go to the cemetery today, would you mind taking some flowers for me? I'll send you some money for them."

"No problem," I said. I pulled a handkerchief out of my pocket to wipe my nose. One of Mama's old handkerchiefs. The one with daisies on it. "And don't worry about the money."

"Thank you," she said. "I'll send you a check anyway. Know that I'm thinking about you."

"You too," I said. "Give my love to Phil and the kids."

We said good-bye. Then I sat down, put my head on the table, and wept.

Nancy let me off early again today since business at the store has been so slow. With this drought, no one is buying anything for their yard, and I've adopted as many of the plants as I can. I feel bad for them, like the stray dogs that get left behind at the shelter while their kennel-mates go to good families.

When I brought home several flats of flowers earlier in the summer, I planted them in special places in my beds and gave them lots of fertilizer, but the heat started soon after, before they had time to get established. Every day I've fought to keep their leaves from curling and their tips from drooping.

Even the ones I planted for Rose and Mama are suffering. Nancy helped me pick out the most beautiful shade plants—bleeding heart and hosta and astilbe and Japanese painted fern—and I planted them under the protection of the pergola. But even the shade isn't sheltering them this year, now that all their reserves are gone.

When I came home from the shop and the cemetery, I started to sweat just getting from the car to the screen door. I pushed the hair out of my eyes, filled the bowl on the porch with water for the gray barn cat and her kittens, then changed into shorts and a T-shirt and sat in the cool of the kitchen for a minute before going out to water the flowers again.

Some of the plants are making a feeble attempt to bloom, but they need all the energy they can muster just to soak up the water from the hose and try to stay upright. The truth is, there's no substitute for rain, and these rescued plants haven't had a drop of it since I brought them home.

It's like the last day of Mama's life. No matter what I did, I couldn't get her enough pain medicine. Now I can't give the flowers the water they need. It's never enough. They're trying to keep up, but I can't restore their vitality, just like I couldn't restore Mama's. Or Rose's.

Every day I've half expected Nancy to droop from the strain herself, but she doesn't. She puts up her hair in a long, shiny brown ponytail and wears the green polo shirt with NANCY'S FLOWERS on the pocket, and she always makes the best of it.

"No customers, no sales—it means I only have to balance the cash register once a day," she told me last week. I remember having that kind of attitude. Cheerfully forging on, believing that challenges are just temporary and good times will return.

I've tried to stay busy at the shop, dusting the watering cans and rain gauges, rearranging the bird feeders, straightening the bags of mulch and fertilizer. It has given me plenty of time to think, and my thoughts always turn in the same direction:

I think I'm done.

I've tried to journal about those words before, but they never would come out on paper. But now I'm ready to speak them out loud, at least to myself. If I have twenty days to make sense of my life, this is a good place to start.

I think I'm done. I've heard those words over and over, floating up from somewhere inside me like a butterfly. When I first started hearing them a few weeks ago, I sat down and asked myself, "What am I done *with*? Do I want a different job? A new house? Am I done worrying about when the drought will end?"

The answer was always no.

Then I started feeling tired. I know this is how Mama felt toward the end of her life. "I'm weary," she'd say to me. I tended to her with the same care as she'd always given Holly and me. Mama's tinkly laugh was gone, but we still told jokes and stories.

We'd been together for years, ever since Joe left and Mama started forgetting things. Up until then, she'd always had more energy than I did, so I could tell when her health started failing. She slept more, and sometimes she said she was so tired she could hardly move.

Lately I know how she must have felt. I find myself being forgetful, too. I'll pay for my groceries at Ted's Market but accidentally leave a bag behind. Or I'll get home and neglect to take the bags out of the car. I threw out a dozen eggs after they'd spent a sweltering afternoon and entire night in the trunk.

"Menopause," Holly says. "You'll grow out of it." But I'm not sure. The last thing this world needs is another old lady with Alzheimer's and no children to take care of her.

At my last checkup, the doctor told me I'm healthy as a

horse. I asked myself if I was depressed and decided that, except for wishing I had the energy to paint my bathroom, I have nothing to complain about. But at fifty-five years old, without Rose or Mama to care for and with a yard full of plants that I can't bring back to health, I feel like my job is finished.

A few days ago, on a particularly slow day, Nancy put a sign on the door that said, BACK AT 1:00, and we headed down the street to get a sandwich for lunch. We sat in the booth by the window, and I looked out at the neighborhood shops, the same ones I've known my whole life. The fabric shop where Mama bought cotton prints for the dresses she made for me and Holly. The dime store where we shopped for Rose's art supplies for school.

"Are you okay?" Nancy asked. "It seems like you haven't been yourself lately."

"Sure," I said, "just a little tired." The truth was, I hardly had the energy to eat. I'd been thinking about how much I missed my life. Missed desire. Missed the feeling of deliciousness and anticipation keeping me awake at night. I've had a child, a marriage, a job I enjoy. I'm a member of the Five Gallon Club for donating blood so many times. But what am I going to do for the next thirty or forty years? I wished some big, clanging noise would let us know when it's time to go. The end.

Just then, a waitress at the other end of the diner dropped a tray of plates, and the crash resounded through the restaurant. I knew in that moment. When our waitress came to take my plate away, I said, "Thank you. I'm done."

So that's it, I thought to myself that night as I brushed my teeth. *I'm tired. I miss Mama and Rose. And Daddy. I've done the work I came here to do. I'm done.*

That's when I saw the swirls of colored lights that I hadn't seen since I was a child, and I remembered the green pearls in the bottle at the back of the freezer.

DAY TWO

I woke up this morning feeling rested, like I'd had a long and deep sleep. It felt even better than a couple of nights ago, when I stretched out on top of Mama's quilt and slept until dawn. That was from depression. This was from peace.

As the sun came up, I lay on my back and watched the ceiling fan blades spin above as I slowly came out of it, and then I remembered the green pearls. I'd actually done it. I waited for a moment to see if shock waves were going to go through my body, but none did. I lay in bed remembering what rest felt like, maybe for the first time in months. Was it because of the pearls? Because I only have nineteen more days of heat and fatigue? Can it really be that easy? Or am I blocking out the reality?

Making decisions has not always been my strong suit. Especially a decision as important as this one. But I feel calmed by it, as though I've finally decided my future instead of life deciding it for me. It's the same sense of peace I had the night Joe proposed.

I got up, took down the mantel clock from Daddy's bookcase, and wound it as usual. Then I put on some coffee, put out food for the mama cat and kittens, and checked the temperature. Seventy-six degrees already. I sat on the porch with my coffee and looked at the brown leaves on the trees. They were so dry that when I watched the birds at the feeder, I could hear a crackling rustle as they landed on the branches.

Everything dies, I thought to myself, feeling justified in my decision. Suddenly it occurred to me that someone might label this suicide. The thought surprised me, and I felt a wave of guilt.

No, I thought, willing that feeling away. *I've only accelerated my death. Just like if I smoked a pack of cigarettes a day. Everything dies. This is the cycle everything goes through.*

I looked at the flowers, which typically would be bursting with color and vitality at this point in the summer. *The drought accelerated their cycle of death this year,* I thought. *It's a natural occurrence. I'm just doing the same thing. For them it was the drought. For me it's the pearls. It would have happened eventually anyway.*

I'm at peace with that. I don't think God will judge me. Not when I miss Mama and Rose so much.

It's hard to think about Rose without memories of Joe right beside her. He knew her better than I did because they were so much alike. Practical, levelheaded. Rose may have looked like a princess with that thick, long, blond hair, but she would have traded a trip to Disney World for camping with her dad any day.

I thought Mama's love of flowers would pass right on through me to Rose, but our girl was all about bugs instead. Spiders, worms, caterpillars—she collected them in baby food jars that Holly gave us. Rose and Joe would go out at night to dig in the flower beds—always with Rose's dog, Cricket, tagging along—and come up with a new crop. Then she'd fly into the house to show me her latest specimens.

"Mom, look," she said one night when I was baking cupcakes for her Sunday school class. She brought a jar of worms over to the counter where I was spooning the batter into the pans. She teased out a worm and put it on her finger.

"It's green," she said. "Dad said it's wearing camouflage. Isn't it cute?"

Cute wasn't the word I would have used. Especially when the worm fell off her finger and into one of the cupcakes.

I made a noise somewhere between "yuck" and a rhyming expletive. But Rose just laughed, reached into the batter, pulled out the worm, and said, "Come back here, you little rebel," and took it outside to clean it off in the grass.

I looked at Joe across the kitchen with obvious exasperation. But he just smiled that coy smile of his, got a glass out of the cupboard for water, and said, "You know, in most parts of the world, bugs are an essential part of the daily diet."

"Fine," I said, happy to play along. I took the muffin cup with the contaminated batter out of the pan, handed it to Joe, and said, "Enjoy yourself."

"Hey, thanks," he said, not missing a beat. He took it outside, and from my view out the window, I could see him and Rose licking that muffin cup clean.

That's what I mean. Two peas in a pod. I can't say I felt jealous of the bond between them. In fact, I kind of marveled at it. I remember one night, washing dishes and watching them walk back into the hills on one of their scavenger hunts. They each wore a headlamp and carried a miniature spade and bucket. When they disappeared into the valley, into that magic light of dusk, I was almost overcome with contentment. I wondered how I could be so blessed, finding everything I ever wanted in the two people I loved most.

* * *

All the way into town this morning, I stewed about what to tell Nancy. Did I need to tell her anything?

We had one of the slowest days ever at the store. Just another Wednesday. Usually we'd be selling all sorts of fall bulbs and fertilizer this time of year. But everyone's waiting until there's some sign of rain.

A customer came in carrying some half-dead hosta plants. "I bought these last spring," she said. "I need to return them. They're guaranteed."

"Did you plant them in the shade?" I said, guessing she'd never checked to see what conditions they needed.

"Well, sort of," she said.

Yeah, I thought. *You probably burned them alive.* I was just about to say something when Nancy intervened.

"Certainly," she said. "We're happy to give you a refund."

I stepped back and finished dusting the shelf of garden books while the customer pocketed the cash.

"How could you be so accommodating to her?" I asked Nancy after the woman left. "Doesn't she know that everybody's plants are dying this summer? It's not our fault it's a hundred degrees with no rain."

"But the customer's always right," Nancy said.

"Yeah," I said, "even when they don't pay any attention to the laws of nature."

But even daft customers couldn't shake my sense of calm today. I worked harder than ever, but it seemed effortless. I rearranged the window display and cleaned out the back room. Then I swept everywhere except around the floral design counter, where our florist, Betty, was snipping stems and muttering under her breath, trying to get several arrangements ready to go. I know better than to interfere when Betty's in her zone, but she did let me carry the bouquets—five for a funeral and two for a fortieth anniversary—out to the van.

It felt a little like the weeks before I gave birth to Rose—a compulsion to make things neat and tidy, a nesting instinct to prepare a place for what's to come.

At one point, I was alone in the shop. Nancy had gone down the street for lunch, and Betty was making her deliveries. I reveled in the solitude of the back room, straightening up the bundles of baby's breath and stems of dried eucalyptus and singing at the top of my voice. I felt like something mischievous in me had been unleashed. I even danced a little. Then I heard the bell ring, signaling someone had come into the store.

Suddenly I felt embarrassed, wondering if the customer had heard me. I brushed off my pants and went out to the front desk, where two cheerleaders from Lincoln High were waiting.

"Hi, girls," I said. "How can I help you?"

"We're selling sponsorships for the football team," the girl with dreadlocks said. "Nancy bought a sponsorship last year, and we're hoping she'd like to renew."

So confident. Was I ever that confident at their age?

I called Nancy on her cell, got her approval, and filled out the paperwork.

"When does school start?" I asked.

"In two weeks," the blonde said.

"It's changed a little since I went there," I said. "Back in the Dark Ages." The girls giggled.

"You're not *that* old," the girl with dreads said. "Do you have kids who go there? Maybe we know them."

"No," I said. Rose would have graduated years ago, but I didn't tell them that.

"There you go," I said, finishing up the agreement. "Hope you have a great season." It struck me that I wouldn't be around to watch the Friday night sports reports to see how they did.

"Thank you," they said in unison. "Tell Nancy thanks

for us, too." Then they bounced out of the store the way teenagers do, as though they have springs in their shoes.

I resumed my work in the back room, keeping my voice down as I sang this time, and thought about what I'd say to Nancy when she returned. As much as I love the shop, it's not where I want to spend my last days when I have so many things to take care of. And she doesn't need me here, not when it's so slow.

I'd just finished sweeping when Nancy found me in the back room.

"Wow, everything looks amazing," she said. "How did you get all this done?"

"A burst of energy, I guess," I told her.

"Well, thank you. It hasn't looked this good back here for as long as I can remember."

She had picked up a bag of trash to take to the Dumpster when I said, "I've been thinking." She stopped and looked at me.

"I haven't been feeling the best lately," I said.

"Oh?" she said, immediately concerned. "Anything wrong?"

"Not really," I said. "I think it's just this time of year. When Mama died. It's been five years."

"Oh, that's right," Nancy said. "I'm so sorry."

"Well, I'm wondering . . . what would you think if I took a few days off? I wouldn't ask if I thought it would put you in a bind, but things are pretty slow on my end. . . ."

Nancy smiled. "Actually," she said, "that would be more than fine. I was going to ask *you* if we could cut back on your hours for a couple of weeks, until things pick up again. Especially now that you've got things in such good shape. It would really help the balance sheet this month. So, absolutely. Take the time you need. Betty and I can handle things for a while."

"Thank you, Nancy."

She reached out and gave me a hug.

"You've got it, sweetie. Let me know if there's anything I can do," she said.

"You're already doing it," I told her. "This is more than enough."

I gathered up my things to leave, took one last look around the shop, and pinched a leaf off the African violet on the counter. Getting rid of that one dead leaf made the whole plant look so much better.

The day six years ago when I went to see Dr. Edelman, I could hardly see the road for all the sleet. Mid-March, high winds, with shards of ice falling from the sky that stung where they hit bare skin.

I hurried through the parking lot of the clinic, pulling my beige coat collar up around my neck and trying to keep my umbrella, useless against the sleet, from turning inside out. I stood in the entryway, shook out the umbrella, and ran my fingers through my hair, which had turned into ringlets in the rain. Then I approached the reception desk.

"I'm here to see Dr. Edelman," I told the nurse.

"Certainly," the nurse said. "And have you been here before?"

"Yes," I said, "I'm here about my mother. Dr. Edelman said he would see me."

She led me to Dr. Edelman's office—a neat, spare space with big windows that would have been bright on a sunnier day. They faced the north, so sleet spat against them.

Tall and thin, Dr. Edelman had a pointed chin and glasses and salt-and-pepper hair. His lab coat looked like it had been pressed, and his voice was low and soothing. It reminded me of the radio commentators we listened to when we were little.

A bouquet of flowers sat on his desk, a contrast to the angry sky outside the window.

"Thanks so much for seeing me," I said.

"No problem," he said with that deep, gravelly voice. "I've been taking care of your mom for a long time. I'm happy to do whatever I can."

"I know this is odd," I said, "but I have to ask. With your voice, have you ever been on the radio?"

He smiled and shook his head. "No, but you're not the first to ask me that. Years ago a local station interviewed me about being a medic in the war. But that was my last radio appearance."

He leaned forward, ready to change the subject. "So," he said, "tell me how your mother's doing."

"She's going downhill," I said. "Every day it seems like she fades a little more. And she's having more pain. It's getting harder for me to take care of her. She's started having accidents, and she's getting less mobile. It frustrates her so much, and I don't know how to help her."

The doctor nodded.

"And the other day, for the first time, she didn't know who I was," I said, taking a breath. "I want to help her and I don't know how," I repeated.

I looked at my hands, trying to distract myself so I wouldn't cry. I glanced around the office at the diplomas on the wall, the photos of Dr. Edelman's family, a photo of him in uniform, clearly taken when he was much younger.

"When did you serve?" I asked, wishing the change in conversation would make my problem go away.

"The early seventies, in Vietnam," he said, leaning back in his chair. "It's not a time I care to remember."

"But you've got the photo," I said. "Doesn't that remind you?"

"Yes," he said. "I may not want to remember, but I can't forget it, either."

He leaned toward me and put his arms on the desk, suddenly serious. "I don't know if you're aware, but your mother has always been one of my favorite patients," he said. "She's one of the most gracious women I've ever met. She used to bring flowers when she came in for her check-ups. I've never had another patient do such a thing."

"Yes," I said. "That's why I'm desperate, doctor. She doesn't deserve this. She won't leave the house, we can't afford a nursing home, but I don't think I can keep caring for her. The home health aide does what she can, but Mama's in more and more pain. And with the dementia, I'm afraid to leave her alone for more than a minute. Plus, there's something else. . . . She said the other day that she doesn't want to be here any longer."

Dr. Edelman leaned back in his chair again and looked at the Vietnam photo on the shelf. In the image, he wore a camouflage helmet and glasses. He sat on the back of a truck with rice fields behind him. Expressionless. Just a moment in time.

Without looking at me, he said, "I may have something that could help as a last resort."

"What is it?" I asked, feeling slight hope.

He continued staring out the window as though recalling a battle in his mind. "Let me give it some thought," he said, "and I'll get back to you later today."

He turned his chair, sighed, and looked at me with compassion.

"Will that be all right?" he asked.

"Yes. I think my cell phone number is in my mom's file."

"If you don't mind, I'd like to have it handy," he said.

He jotted it down on a slip of paper and tucked it in his pocket.

"Thank you," I said, slipping on my coat.

"You're welcome. I'll get back to you this afternoon."

The next morning, Mama was still sleeping when Dr. Edelman came to the back door, carrying a small black bag. True to his word, he'd called me three hours after I left his office. It surprised me to get a call directly from him—not from a nurse or assistant.

He asked if he could drop something off for me at the house. It was the first time I could remember a doctor making a house call since Daddy had pneumonia a few months before his accident.

"Sit down," I said. "Would you like some coffee?" I wasn't quite sure how to host a doctor.

"No, thank you," he said, setting the bag on the table. "I won't be here long. How's your mother this morning?"

"She seems to sleep well at this time of day," I said. "It makes up for the fitful sleep she has in the middle of the night."

"That's very common," Dr. Edelman said as he turned the silver clasp on his bag. "Is the medication she's been on helping at night?"

"A little, yes."

He reached into the bag and pulled out a small cooler. Inside, packed in ice, sat a small white bottle without a label. It looked odd for a pharmaceutical bottle. The only markings were numerals stamped on the side: 20.

"Twenty," I said. "What does that mean?"

"That's the code we used in the military," the doctor said. He took the bottle, unscrewed the cap, and opened it. Inside were a dozen little green frozen pearls, like small drops of gelatin.

"I'm going to give these to you, but I want to be clear about them," he said. "Use them only if you see a dramatic change in your mother, if her pain is unmanageable. They're tasteless, but they're easiest to administer in yogurt or ice cream. Just mix them in. They'll dissolve when they come in contact with anything."

"And what do they do?" I asked, not sure I wanted to know.

"They'll make her feel much better," he said, then paused. "And on the twentieth day, she'll pass on peacefully."

I took a deep breath, trying to understand the power of what I held in my hand.

"So they're lethal," I said. My voice sounded monotone, the same way Dr. Edelman's had the day before. "You're giving me something to kill my own mother."

"I think of it as life-giving," Dr. Edelman said. "They'll make her final days more comfortable and will give her a peaceful passing into the life beyond this body. And they'll restore your life, as well. You won't have to see her suffer needlessly."

I stared at the bottle. "Why twenty days?" I asked.

"I can't tell you for sure," Dr. Edelman said. "They were developed so they couldn't be detected. After twenty days, they trigger a complete and peaceful shutdown of the heart."

I stood, silent. Part of me wanted to throw the bottle at him and tell him to leave. But I didn't.

"This is one complete dose," he said. "It needs to be taken all at once. Give it to her just before bed, and she'll pass in her sleep twenty nights later."

I felt chills going through my body. Not so much chills of fear as the chills of truth. I knew I should be outraged and appalled at the power in those green pearls, but instead I felt grateful, even humbled, as though I stood in the presence of something sacred.

"And you know for sure that they work?" I asked.

Dr. Edelman nodded. "I've used them only in extreme cases, of course. But sometimes helping people cross that threshold from pain to peace is the greatest gift you can give them."

"You're sure they can't be traced?" I said. "What if there's an autopsy?"

"Don't worry," he said. His soothing voice comforted me. "They turn off the control centers in the brain, and it looks as though the patient has had a heart attack."

I took a deep breath. "Are you certain there's no pain?"

"Believe me," he said, "I saw enough people die horrible deaths in the war. I wouldn't ever want to inflict that kind of pain on anyone. This is the most peaceful passing you could give your mom—if she needs that help."

I glanced toward Mama's bedroom, wondering if I'd ever seriously think of using them. At the same time, nothing in me wanted to give the bottle back.

"Thank you," I said.

"Of course," Dr. Edelman said. He put his hand on my shoulder. "You need to make sure no one knows, and that no one gets into the bottle accidentally. Keep it in the freezer until you need it."

"Do they expire?"

"Apparently not," Dr. Edelman said. "I've had these for years. You'll know they're working because they kill the virus that causes moles and warts. They clear up age spots and other blemishes, as well."

"Wish I'd had them for my acne when I was a teenager," I said, trying to cut the tension.

Dr. Edelman smiled. "I know it seems like you're playing God," he said. "But we play God every day when we give people medications or surgeries to keep them alive. Sometimes the more loving thing is to let them go."

I nodded, aware of how cold the bottle felt in my hand. "Thank you," I said again.

"Let me know if you need anything," Dr. Edelman said. He put the empty cooler back in his black bag, turned the clasp closed, and left.

DAY THREE

This morning I woke up with a tingling sensation in my feet. It didn't last long, but I sat up in bed, swung my feet over the side, and massaged them. It's not a feeling I've ever had before, and like every little sensation in my body now, I'm wondering if it's the pearls at work. The thought doesn't make me unhappy. In fact, just the opposite. There's a little exhilaration. A quickening, a feeling that I'm coming closer to what I've wanted for a long, long time, even though I'd never considered taking the pearls before.

The tingling didn't last long. By the time I got up, wound the clock, fed the cats, and watered the flowers, I didn't notice it anymore, and it hasn't come back. A good thing, too, since I had plenty to do today, getting started on the long list I posted on the refrigerator door last night.

I've been a chronic list-maker my whole life. It gives me some illusion that my life is under control or I can foresee the immediate future. Whenever my mind starts feeling like the desk catch-all drawer—a scattered mess of paper clips, broken rulers, and old pens—writing things down makes me feel like I've cleared out the clutter, at least momentarily. Sometimes I've written *Take a shower* or *Brush teeth* on the list just so I can feel productive. I've even added items to the list after I've done them so I could cross them off.

Joe used to tease me about my obsessiveness, adding his own notes to my list when I wasn't around. *Open eyes when you wake up in the morning,* he wrote one time. *Breathe in. Breathe out.* Or *Crack eggs before scrambling them.*

"Very funny," I told him one day after breakfast when I discovered his latest notes.

"Just trying to help," he said, smiling. He started backing out of the room, expecting me to chase him with the spatula I was holding.

"Oh," he said, "and don't forget to take off the gas cap before you fuel up the car." Then he turned and sprinted out the door. Next thing I knew he and Rose were laughing and chasing each other out in the yard, and Cricket was barking to high heaven.

I've never made a list like this before. It's all the things I need to do in the next seventeen days. The house needs a good cleaning, but not just surface stuff. I want to get rid of all the excess items so Holly won't have to go through them after I'm gone. Old clothes, old papers, stacks of books, extra plates and dishes.

I'll leave what's left of Mama's things, but anything that belongs to me will find a new home. I remember what a huge job Holly and I had after Mama died. Days of sorting and making piles, taking truckloads to Goodwill, packing up boxes for Holly to take back to Seattle, pitching stuff or burning old papers in the burn barrel out back.

"I'm never buying another thing," I said to Holly while we sorted. "We've all got enough for three lifetimes." Holly felt the same way, but some items were too precious to give up. She shipped home a cut-glass vase that Mama and

Daddy received as a wedding gift and a painted plate that Mama used for serving her famous coconut cake when we were little.

My intention is to make my passing as quiet and easy for everyone else as it is for me. Stirring the pearls into my yogurt certainly was simple enough, like eating a bowl of ice cream with topping. I intend for the rest of the seventeen days to be just as simple—and for the days afterward, with Holly taking care of things, to be equally so. I can't tell anyone what I've done or I'll set off a chain reaction of panic and trying to find a way to reverse the effect of the pearls. But I can make it easy for my sister after I'm gone.

I tried to calculate when the passing might happen on the twentieth day. If Dr. Edelman was right, I'd pass at about 3:30 a.m. Just go to bed early that night and not wake up. Somehow I'll need to arrange for someone to find me. Another thing for the list. Ask someone to come over on the twenty-first day. Not an easy thing for anyone to do, but better than waiting until Nancy wonders why I never came back to work.

In all the to-do lists I'd ever made, I had never expected to write, *Arrange for someone to find my body.*

But what if the pearls work faster? Slower? Or not at all? They were years old, after all. I guess in that way, my situation is not so different from how we ordinarily live and die. We don't know exactly when the end will come.

If the pearls work, I have seventeen days to get my life in order once and for all. I find a certain peace in that. No big ambitions or goals. No bucket list with items to be crossed off. I'm not going to try to wedge in a hot air balloon ride and a trip to Nepal.

My bucket list is more about a cleaning bucket. What can I clear up and get rid of? What can I wash down and spruce up?

Just drag all the old and broken refuse of life off to the

dump and recycling center, redeem my soda cans and wine bottles, delete the old e-mails on my computer, and make sure my financial affairs are in order.

I wouldn't take the time to do this for myself. But I'll do it for Holly. I don't want her to deal with a mess once I'm gone.

So here's my "bucket" list:

- Clean out the refrigerator and freezers (defrost the chest freezer)
- Get rid of junk in the shed
- Check in with friends and neighbors
- Organize photos
- Delete old e-mails
- Go through the basement storage room
- Organize all financial paperwork and make a list of account numbers and passwords
- Review my will
- Throw out old toiletries and cleaning supplies
- Take clothes to Goodwill
- Clean out the glove compartment
- Sweep out the garage
- Pare down old books and magazines—take them to the library

After I wrote out the list, I pulled the Animal Rescue League calendar out of the kitchen drawer and hung it on the wall. I marked red Xs on the last couple of days, counted out to twenty, and circled that date.

August 28.

I took in a little breath of air. That was the day I met Joe, all those many years ago.

It's hard to believe how life sneaks up on you and ac-cumulates until you don't even know how buried you are in the past, how much it encroaches on the present, and squeezes all the energy out of it.

I started cleaning the closets and drawers, which seemed less intimidating than the attic and shed. Usually I'd use the trinity plan to sort things: Pitch, Donate, or Sell. But I eliminated the Sell because there's no need. Either something has value and I'll take it to Goodwill, or it has fulfilled its purpose and it's time to let go.

As I went through the closets, I wished I could have always been this decisive. The coatdress from Cousin Georgia's wedding thirteen years ago? Gone. The boots with the heels I could never walk in? Gone. No more second-guessing myself, thinking I might wake up one day and regret getting rid of the embroidered Christmas sweater with a big chenille pom-pom for Rudolph's nose.

Then I got to Mama's clothes. There aren't a lot of them, but I couldn't bring myself to give them all away when she died. Her garden pants. Her flowered robe. Everyone knew Mama as the Flower Lady. At the height of her gardening days, her flower beds were legendary. In June, an entire bed of purple larkspur and coral-pink gaillardia filled the space next to the shed, attracting strangers who came just to stand and stare. The colors were so vibrant, it seemed as though Mama had planted varieties of her own making.

The visitors had the same look on their faces that Joe and I had when we went to New York years ago and came face-to-face with a real van Gogh painting. I remember the feeling of reverence, and how I could see the colors of van Gogh's flowers reflected in Joe's face as he drank them in.

Every year for Memorial Day, the peonies on the south side of Mama's house were so fragrant you could smell them as soon as you stepped out on the porch. And in the fall, the brown-eyed Susans and autumn clematis filled up the bed. The clematis, with its tiny white blooms growing up Mama's trellis, looked like something a bride would wear as a veil.

Mama started entering flowers in the State Fair at the age of thirteen, and she never stopped except when she judged the floral competition. In the attic years ago, I found three huge boxes of ribbons she'd won. Before her dementia started to advance, I asked her what she'd like to have done with them, and she waved away the question like it didn't matter.

"Oh, all those ribbons," she said. "The ribbons don't matter much . . . never did. The important part was growing the flowers and somehow being a part of all that beauty. And entering them in the competition felt like a way to share them. Those ribbons are no tribute to my talent. . . . They're about what nature can do."

I'll let Holly decide what to do with them, but I put a note on one of the boxes that they could be donated to the State Fair for their archives. Mama brought so much beauty to this world; she deserves to live on.

I walked down to the mailbox to get the mail after I watered the flowers for the second time today. The corners of two envelopes stuck out from the rest. One was a bank statement, the other the gas bill. *Won't have to worry about these much longer,* I thought as I walked back up the gravel lane toward the house.

Inside, I added notes to my bucket list: *Pay all bills, bring everything up-to-date, organize my records so that when Holly comes to settle things after I'm gone, it will be as easy on her as possible.*

I sat down at the kitchen table, kicked off my sandals, put one leg up under me, and wiped away the condensation on the glass of iced tea I'd poured. I glanced through the rest of the mail, stopping when I came to a nondescript white envelope. The handwriting was almost as familiar as my own. A note from Joe.

It didn't really surprise me. I tore it open and pulled out a simple card picturing a watercolor of wildflowers. *Thinking of you,* it said. Inside, he'd written, *I know this is a hard time of year.*

Joe always sends a card around the time of Mama's passing. It's a sweet gesture. I suppose he does it for the same reason he came to her funeral. "I thought of her as my mama, too, you know."

He used to spend hours helping her in the barn, which she called the "international headquarters" for her antiques and furniture repair business. She was a self-taught seamstress, upholsterer, refinisher, and woodworker.

Daddy had left behind a workbench full of tools, and Mama had learned the value of making do from her own mother. Those assets, along with the necessity of feeding two daughters, were enough to prompt a business that kept the mortgage and dental bills paid until Holly and I went to college.

Mama did yoga before anyone else around here had heard of it. Too old to be a hippie, she was an earth mother, an early adopter of lentil casseroles and bean sprouts that she grew in old Mason jars on the top of our refrigerator.

Her workshop for the antiques business smelled of turpentine and wood stain, a combination both pungent and sweet. When she was refinishing a piece of furniture that had seen better days, she wore a carpenter's apron with a pocket across the front for her tools. Each day when she took off the apron, she shook out the sawdust, snapping it just like our sheets used to snap in the wind on the clothesline, and hung it on a hook by the door.

Often when she stood by a table or chest of drawers,

brushing stain across the velvety sanded surface, she adopted the yoga Tree Pose, holding one foot up against the opposite leg with perfect balance. She was so steady that she could switch from one leg to the other without the slightest bobble. She did this when she cooked, too, if she stood at the stove for a long time, stirring a cream soup or a batch of fudge.

Mama even—and this embarrasses and inspires me yet today—created her own walking Tree Pose while she was cooking or tidying up around the house. She stood with one foot up. Put it down. Took a step. Put the other foot up. Put it down. She could vacuum the entire house that way without missing a beat.

We called her the Ostrich. And we told no one. No one could know this odd and wonderful secret about our mom.

Of course, Joe found out. The first time he saw her do the ostrich walk, he laughed so hard he literally doubled over. "Lillian, you are a wonder," he said when he finally composed himself. "Will you teach me how to do it?"

We spent a lot of Saturdays at Mama's after we were married. I'd tend to the yard work while Joe helped her build legs for a tabletop she found by the side of the road or flip over a couch so she could finish tacking its skirt in place.

They'd listen to Cubs games and Cyclone games and whatever else was in season. And they'd feed carrots to Romeo, the docile horse Mama started boarding as another source of income when we were in high school.

Romeo's owners came to our house just often enough to keep him happy. Then, when they moved away, they sold him to Mama for almost nothing, along with a trailer, bridle, and saddle. Holly and I were never horse crazy, but we were glad Mama had Romeo to talk to when Joe wasn't around.

Mama always said she loved Joe like a son. He'd give her

a big bear hug whenever we saw her, and he filled that hole that had been gaping open for so many years since Daddy died.

"Lillian," he'd say, "you're the mom I always wished I had." He considered her "one of his girls," just like Rose and me.

Mama had a hard time when we got divorced. She never said much about it because she knew how much pain I was in, but she blamed me, I know. And rightly so.

I've never been in love with anyone else. I couldn't imagine starting a relationship with someone new. I dated occasionally after Mama passed away, but I've always been dismal at small talk, and I learned pretty quickly that most men got tense if I talked honestly about my life.

Joe and I were always so comfortable together. Even after all these years, that's what I remember. After our divorce, going out with a man who felt like a stranger and asking about his work and his hobbies felt exhausting. I came home feeling lonelier than I already was.

Joe and I met in college two weeks into my junior year. He worked in the student union café serving greasy french fries and Folgers coffee. I went there every Tuesday and Thursday after my horticulture lab and sat at the same table in a corner that smelled of old textbooks. I never could tolerate chaos, but at this time of the morning the place was quiet, and it made me feel connected to people after spending time with the plants.

I'd noticed Joe from a distance before. His sandy hair, slim build, the way he lingered at students' tables after delivering their food to ask if they needed anything else. He didn't hurry. I marveled at his peculiar combination of effortlessness and efficiency.

He'd never waited on me before. But when I looked up

from my plant identification book, there he stood with a pot of coffee in his hand, his eyes so much bluer than they seemed from a distance.

"Would you like a refill?" he asked. "It's a fresh pot. I made it myself."

"Sure," I said, noticing his name tag. Joe Mitchell. "Do you do the cooking *and* serving?" I asked.

"Sometimes," he said. "Depends on whether the regular cook partied too much the night before."

"Oh," I said, opening a packet of sugar and stirring it into my mug. "So you're the one they can count on."

"Guess so," he said, smiling. "Let me know if you need anything else, okay?"

It didn't take long for me to figure out I needed *him*. From that day on, he made a point of waiting on me, and every time, our conversations grew. He was a senior, an engineering major. He'd interned with the state during the summer, working on bridges and a new dam.

I didn't need to hear much more before I felt myself falling. Even though I was little when Daddy died, his legacy of making things lived on in me. An artist or dreamer held no attraction. I needed a man who knew how to fix and build and repair. I searched for it without even knowing.

Joe knew how to build our relationship. He proposed to me on a camping trip in Minnesota, when we were in a canoe out in the middle of a lake. We sat in the light of the moon, listening to the loons calling and the water gently lapping around our oars. "You're my best friend," he said. "Would you do me the honor of being my wife?"

I felt a surge of joy as big as the night sky when he put the ring on my finger. Then we almost capsized the canoe when he leaned over to kiss me.

He knew how to make me laugh, even after the third miscarriage, when we almost gave up on having children.

And he knew how to be the father to Rose that I'd always wanted. But after she was gone, it seemed that our marriage was held together by death rather than life.

The night Joe left, I didn't even cry, which shows how empty I felt inside.

He wasn't angry when he walked out. Neither of us slammed a door or threw a glass against the wall.

At supper that night, I'd said these words: "I think I need some time alone."

He put his fork down, sat back in his chair, and nodded. Then he got up, went to the bedroom, and packed a suitcase.

Fifteen minutes later, he kissed me on the forehead, said, "I hope you find what you're looking for," and walked through the door.

I pulled my sweater tighter around me, went to bed, and didn't get up for fourteen hours. Days passed before I cried, feeling the earth slip out from under me. He was the man I'd trusted for twenty years, the only one who knew Rose as I did, who shared my history with me. It was hard enough to accept that he'd left.

It was so much harder to know I'd pushed him away.

Mama's funeral five years ago took place on a warm day, not sweltering like this year. Joe flew out from California, and I saw him face-to-face for the first time in seven years.

"How are Carol and the kids?" I asked, wanting him to say they were terrible and that he'd made a big mistake.

"Good," he said, looking around the room at all the faces from his past. And then he quickly changed the subject. "I think the whole town is here, don't you?" he asked.

They were. Everyone had turned out. All those people who had sat in our kitchen, enjoying a cup of coffee and Mama's coconut cake, all the ones she'd stood beside, serving church suppers and making quilts. All her friends from childhood who still lived nearby, and some who had come from other states.

It meant a lot to me that Joe came for the funeral. I certainly never asked him to. In fact, I wasn't sure how he knew about Mama, until Holly confessed.

"He e-mails me every once in a while," she said. "Just checking in, a friendly hello. But he and Mama used to be so close, I knew he'd want to know. I hope you don't mind," she said.

"No, you were right to tell him," I said, studying him across the room as he talked with some of our old neighbors. His hair was grayer, but his eyes were still that oceanic blue. He had put on a few pounds, but in a navy-blue suit, he looked trim for his age.

When I first saw him again after so long, my response took me by surprise. I felt butterflies, a lot like when we were dating. Whatever had been dead in me when he'd left seemed to have come alive again. But bad timing, as always. It sounded as if he and Carol and her girls had made a life for themselves. And how could I be angry? Didn't he deserve happiness with someone else since he couldn't have it with me?

Today when I got his card about Mama, I noticed he has a new return address. He and Carol must have moved. *Hard to believe it's been five years since we lost her,* he wrote. *Hope you're doing okay.*

We *lost her,* I thought. Funny that he still thinks of us as "we."

I remember one November day when I was six years old, a year after we buried Daddy. I crossed the half-frozen creek to play with my friend Teresa after school. The sun set early, and when I came back home, the fluorescent light over the kitchen sink welcomed me, but Mama and Holly were gone.

I looked out back. I ran to the shed and called their names. I went in the house and turned on the radio and the TV, just to feel less alone. But I *was* alone. I thought of the children's book where the little boy comes home from school and finds that his family has moved away. No way to reach them, totally adrift. That's how I felt.

Ten minutes later Mama drove up with Holly standing in the backseat of the car, the way we did in those days. They'd run into town for groceries, and it took longer than Mama expected. She felt so bad she let me eat cereal straight out of the box for a week. But it didn't erase how terrified I felt sitting in the kitchen, hearing the evening news, the Top 40 DJ, and the hum of the fluorescent light over the sink, not knowing if I'd see Mama and Holly again.

That's how I've been feeling. I keep thinking of the reasons I took the pearls, and this is one of them. I come home to an empty house, to an overwhelming presence of nothingness. I'm amazed how spirits inhabit a home. When Joe and Rose and I were together, the two of them could be gone for hours, but they still felt as present in the house as if they were sitting in front of the TV or curled up together reading a book on the porch. The house held their conversation and laughter in safekeeping, even if Joe traveled half a world away on a research trip or Rose spent a week at camp.

That's why I knew Rose wouldn't survive her accident. Not because of anything the doctors said or how she looked when she lay so still with a tangle of tubes threaded into her. But because when I walked into the house the first night she was in the hospital, after Mama insisted that Joe and I go home for a while, the house felt empty. Her spirit had left it, as if a huge vacuum had sucked out the air, and I could tell she wasn't coming back.

*   *   *

After Rose died, I went to a grief weekend at the monastery in Parkerville, two hours away. Joe didn't go with me. He said he needed to grieve in his own way.

By the time it was over, I wished I'd stayed home, too. I sat in the stone sanctuary where the monks sang lauds in the morning, in a circle with ten other people who had lost a loved one. All the others were grieving the loss of a spouse. I know how hard that is, but I couldn't help thinking that my situation was different, and no one could truly understand.

Especially Father Xavier. So small he was almost elf-like, with a beatific smile and a bald head. What did a monk know about the loss of a child? Or the loss of a spouse, for that matter?

I remember how heavy the air felt in that room, so stifling I sometimes couldn't breathe. My sadness almost overwhelmed me. What had I been thinking to want to join my despair with others'?

One woman with long fingernails and a silver cross necklace spoke up first. "It's been ten years," she said, kneading a tissue in her hands. She sounded angry, almost defiant. "I still miss my husband as much as ever. I cry for him every single day."

I understand her feelings now, but at the time it felt like a death sentence, being told I would never get over it, that the pain would linger like an open sore.

The retreat was supposed to be about self-care. But how in the world could I tend to myself when I didn't have my daughter to care for?

Father Xavier had an assignment for us: "Write out your pain in letters to God," he said. "Pour it out on paper. Don't hold anything back."

I went to my room, a simple space with a bed and small writing desk and a sink with one towel. I sat down at the desk with paper and a pen and wrote for three hours. It *did* come pouring out—the anger, the hopelessness, the blame, the betrayal, the guilt. I wanted to scream but—and I know how ridiculous this sounds—the monastery had a policy of silence, and I didn't want to break the rules.

Twice I thought I might hurt myself to ease the suffering, but I thought about Joe and Mama, and I went back to the writing.

I finished my letters by quoting the 23rd Psalm, all the pretty language that the minister had read at Daddy's graveside years before. Peace. Love. Healing. I thought of the quote from Philippians about "the peace which passeth all understanding." Like that would ever be possible.

The last thing I wrote was this: *I didn't know until now that God is a vicious liar.*

I put that letter on top.

I found those letters today, wrapped up in red string and buried in a box at the back of the bedroom closet.

They certainly didn't belong in the Donate pile. And somehow I wasn't quite ready to Pitch them, either.

DAY FOUR

When I woke up this morning, I tried to remember the peace of the last few days—the energy and anticipation. But instead I felt a deep sense of dread, as though someone had pinned me to the bed with a knife. I lay frozen and stared at the ceiling, watching the fan blades circle over and over.

What have I done?

I forced myself out of bed, even though I felt as if someone had run me over. Six thirty. Nothing ahead today but more heat. And more cleaning. Endless. It seems endless.

I pulled on a pair of jean shorts and a T-shirt and tried to calm myself as I wound the mantel clock, started a pot of coffee, and put food out for the barn cats.

The heat hit me as I opened the door. I haven't felt this helpless since the ambulance delivered Rose to the hospital. But this is different. I did this. It wasn't an accident; it was my own conscious decision. And now I feel like I'm in a cage and can't get out.

Back inside, I looked at the calendar on the wall, fixated on those glaring red Xs. And then I looked at all the days after. The days I won't see—not if those pearls actually work.

Maybe there's an antidote.

There's an antidote for everything, right? Maybe I can still save myself. But here's the reality: I've taken a substance that's known to be deadly, developed and given to me in secret. I don't know its source, no one is going to want to talk about it, and I'm not supposed to have it. Plus, I could ruin Dr. Edelman's life if I were to reveal the secret, and I don't even know whether the stuff works or if it expired years ago.

Even the bottle—the only physical evidence—is gone. I set it out yesterday with the trash, and it's in a landfill by now.

But finding an antidote was worth a try. In that moment, I decided, I had to try.

I found Dr. Edelman's number in Mama's address book, which I keep in the drawer by her bed, along with three of her old handkerchiefs and one of her favorite brooches. I figured he might be retired, but at least the office could put me in touch with him.

"Dr. Edelman, please," I said into the phone, trying to control my voice.

"Dr. Edelman?" the receptionist asked on the other end of the phone. "Do you mean Dr. Marvin Edelman?"

"Yes," I said.

"I'm sorry," the voice said, "but Dr. Edelman passed away three years ago."

I swallowed hard and took a breath. "I'm sorry," I said. "I didn't know."

I paused as I tried to think of some other tactic, but what would I ask? I couldn't share his secret. Surely he wouldn't have any records.

"Thank you," I said, and hung up the phone.

I sat down at the computer and Googled him. I Googled his name and *20, Twenty, 2.0, Vietnam, lethal agent,* hoping something might come up. Maybe Dr. Edelman had made a deathbed confession. Maybe he'd explained what the stuff was, where he'd gotten it, how it could be reversed.

But all I found was his obituary.

Dr. Marvin Edelman was born May 7, 1941, in Lorimor, Iowa. He attended the University of Iowa College of Medicine and served as a medic in the Vietnam War from 1971 to 1973. Specializing in gerontology, he cared for his patients in family practice for nearly four decades. He retired earlier this year and is survived by his wife, Lucille; three children; and seven grandchildren. Dr. Edelman died peacefully in his sleep after a battle with cancer.

"Died peacefully in his sleep." Had he taken the pearls, too?

They have no idea, I thought as I closed the computer. I sat back and stared out the window at the curling brown leaves on the trees, stunned. I had no idea where to go from here.

Who could I talk to? How would I pose the question? *Maybe you can help me. I've heard of a substance— military, top secret—that will kill you in twenty days. Can you tell me anything about it?*

Who would I call with those questions?

No one. But maybe there was a different way. Maybe the pearls had left a marker within me somehow. Maybe if I had blood drawn, it would show something. At least I might know if the pearls were working or not.

I paused for a moment to get my story straight, then called my doctor's office.

"This is Carla," the nurse said. "May I help you?"

"Yes," I said, trying to sound nonchalant. "I came in for a physical back in June, but we didn't do a full blood workup at the time. Could I come in and have blood drawn for that?"

"Certainly. Are you having symptoms, or do you just want this as a follow-up for your records?"

"Just as a follow-up," I said, grateful she was giving me the right words.

"Sure. Since you don't need to see the doctor, you can come in anytime and I can take care of that for you."

"How about this morning?" I said, feeling a sense of urgency rising in me. "I have some errands to run, so I could stop in."

"Yes, that's fine," she said. "Just ask for me when you get here."

Until I hung up the phone, I didn't realize I was shaking.

I'd calmed down a bit by the time I got to the clinic. Carla greeted me with a clipboard in hand, led me back to an exam room, and closed the door. I looked at the examining table and remembered how many times I'd lain on that table or one like it, hearing the crinkle of the paper beneath me whenever I made the slightest move.

Joe was there for the appointments that confirmed I was pregnant. And he was there for the appointments that confirmed I wasn't any longer. With my fourth pregnancy, he tried to lighten the mood when we went in for my first trimester exam. "You've probably had your feet in more stirrups than Annie Oakley," he said.

Today, I was grateful I wouldn't need the exam table or paper gown. I sat in the chair in the exam room while Carla washed her hands and put on gloves.

"So we're doing a full panel of blood work, right?" she said, applying the tourniquet to my arm.

"Right," I said, feeling the pressure.

"And you're not having any symptoms?"

"Right," I said again, thinking of everything I wasn't saying.

I took some stuff that's supposed to kill me in a few

days, but there's no evidence that it ever existed, and I don't know what it was or what's in it.

That would likely get me thrown in a locked unit for observation and suicide watch. *If it's between that and dying, for all the reasons I took the stuff in the first place, I'll stick with my original plan.*

"Okay," she said as she unwrapped the needle. "You'll feel a little pinch."

I looked away, thinking of all the times I'd given blood with no concern about what was in it. But this blood could be tainted, couldn't it? I have no idea if the lab tests will show anything—or what will happen if they do—but I have to find out.

"How long will it take to get the results?" I said.

"Not long," Carla said. "Let's see. This is Friday. They should be mailed to you early next week."

Can I wait that long? Then again, what choice do I have?

"Let us know if you have any questions when you get the results," Carla said as she walked me out to the waiting area. "They'll tell you if the doctor sees any red flags."

"Thanks," I said, feeling a little light-headed.

Before I left, I stopped in the restroom to splash cold water on my face. That was when I noticed. The age spot under my left eye—the one I've covered up for the last three years—is gone.

Mama always made things look so easy. She put together a meal like magic when people dropped in. She didn't stress over things. Didn't raise a fuss when Holly and I made a mess. A couple of years before she died, I asked her about it while we were doing a jigsaw puzzle, one of her favorite pastimes.

"I learned what was important and what wasn't after your dad died," she said.

"But why haven't I learned it since Rose died?" I said.

"Because losing a spouse is different from losing a child," she said. "When a spouse dies, you lose a partner and your future together. But when a child dies, you lose your trust that the world operates the way it's supposed to."

She searched the puzzle to find where her next piece belonged. "Rose's death defied the laws of nature," she said. "Children aren't supposed to die before their parents."

I kept studying the puzzle pieces for something that might fit.

"The grief process is different because there's so much anger, confusion, and guilt," she said. "When you have a child, you accept an unspoken contract to help that child live and thrive. You'd lay down your life for that child. When your child dies first, there's so much guilt that you didn't fulfill the contract, that it was somehow your fault."

We both kept our eyes on the puzzle.

"But it *was* my fault," I said.

"No, it wasn't," she said. "Remember, I was here when it happened. You did nothing wrong. There's no explanation that will ever satisfy either of us. But it happened. Why, we don't know."

I moved in with Mama when her dementia took hold, and while I despised the thievery of the disease, I loved taking care of her. Even Romeo, who had kept her company out in the barn all those years when she had her antiques business, had passed away of old age—or maybe from a broken heart. Mama needed me. We needed each other.

Each morning I tiptoed into her bedroom, leaned over the bed to breathe in her smell, as familiar to me as childhood, and sat quietly by her bed for a few moments to watch her sleep. I traced the wrinkles around her eyes, the cascade of hair that had once been so full and stylish. Still surprisingly shiny despite the gray.

Mama used to put it up in a bun or wear it loose around

her shoulders. I thought we should cut it to make it easier to care for, but she protested, and I didn't fight her on it. "It's still the part of me I love the most," she said one day, sitting at the kitchen table. "I don't care if it gets in my way."

She used to tell me, "You're young, you should be out having fun with a man. Hell, I'm young. If it weren't for my memory, I'd be out on a date."

But I preferred to stay home and take care of her. I'd come home after work, tired of trying to make customers happy at the shop all day. I got to the point where I didn't return phone calls because chatting about nothing exhausted me. I found all the companionship I needed in the flowers and Mama.

Before the dementia took away all her stories, I recorded our conversations so I could capture her voice and her cadence, and I could picture her, the way she used her hands like big, swooping birds when she talked.

I played games with her; we read to each other. We made place mats and napkins on her old Kenmore sewing machine, which brought back memories of those summer days when she taught me how to sew.

On hot summer mornings when I checked on her, Mama sometimes had one foot sticking out from under the covers. I marveled at how youthful her feet were. Long, slender, smooth, they looked like the feet of a twenty-year-old. Elegant. Regal, even. I imagined that a queen's feet would look this way, or a princess's. And I thought how much our roles had changed. I played the mom now, and Mama the little princess. And I was happy to fulfill any wish she had.

Those wishes were simple, usually. She wanted the TV tray moved closer so she could sit up straighter. She needed a different pillow for reading. She wanted to sit in her favorite spot under the pergola, where it felt cool no matter how hot the summer day.

Often the two of us sat together in the kitchen late in the afternoon after I got home from work. I asked her about her childhood, and about how she and Daddy met.

"I've told you that story a hundred times," Mama would say. "You know exactly how it happened."

I nodded and winked. "Yes," I said, "but I've forgotten the details. Can't you tell me again?"

Mama didn't need much prodding. She told the whole tale again. How they met three years after Daddy came home from Korea. He'd finished college on the GI Bill and started his work as an insurance underwriter. He came to the diner where she waitressed and sat at one of her tables every morning, ordering eggs over easy before he went to work.

"It took him two months to ask me out," Mama said. "I'd get so frustrated. How could I let him know I wanted to go out with him without being too obvious?"

"So what did you do?" I asked. It was part of the script between the two of us, as though we'd rehearsed it many times before.

"I asked my boss to put a different waitress at that table," Mama said, gathering her hair up behind her head like a young girl. "I said hello to him when he came in and then ignored him. It worked like a charm. He asked me out the next day."

"You've always been a wise woman," I said, feeling satisfied to hear the story one more time.

I imagined my parents' early days living in a tiny apartment on the square, buying their first Buick, driving cross country to Yellowstone Park, taking their pictures with a Brownie camera and saving them in a photo album with those little white corner stickers. Mama got nauseous on that trip and blamed it on carsickness. But when they got back home, she found out she was pregnant with me.

"Maybe that's why I always liked the West," I said.

"True enough," said Mama. "You were there in spirit before I even knew you existed."

I heard on the news today that two people have been arrested for animal cruelty because they left their dogs outside in the heat. In both cases, the owners had left bowls of water with the dogs, but with temperatures over 100 degrees for the sixth day in a row, the water got hot and dogs won't drink hot water. I never knew this. Sometimes we have what we need right in front of us, but we're programmed not to let it in.

Maybe that's what happened when Holly called tonight. When I told her I'd decided to take a few days off because of the heat, she invited me to come out and see her.

"The kids would love it," she said, "and so would I. We haven't had real time together for a couple of years now."

I couldn't think what to say, so I stumbled around. "But there's so much I need to do here."

"Like what?" she said.

"Cleaning out closets, doing a little painting." Even as I said it, I knew she'd think it was lame. I tried to make a stronger case by invoking Mama's name. "Sprucing the place up a little. I've been neglecting it a long time. Mama would be wagging her finger at me. . . ."

"Yeah, and then she'd climb up on a ladder and fix it," she said. "But you can do that anytime. Do it in the dead of winter when you're stuck at home for a weekend. How often do you have a week or two of unscheduled time? You deserve to get away. And the kids aren't back in school yet, so we could go to the aquarium, spend some time at the waterfront. It would be great for all of us. They always love spending time with their favorite aunt."

The fact that I'm their *only* aunt is never lost on me

when she says that. A part of me wanted to tell her I'd be there tomorrow, wanted to spill the whole story. But I'm not ready to tell her the truth.

Plus she doesn't know that even though I love the kids, they bring back difficult memories. Rose and the boys used to play together when they were little. Now Mark and Brent are almost out of college, which reminds me that Rose would be well into her adult life by now. Maybe married. Maybe I'd be a grandma.

Anyway, how could I go and stay in Holly's house, not knowing for sure what's going to happen in the next two weeks? Maybe the pearls will kick in sooner, and she'd find me dead in her guest room. Maybe my nervous system will go haywire and I'll have a stroke. Maybe I'll start to turn green and my eyebrows will fall out. The last thing I want to do is to leave her needing to take care of me.

"Another time, Holly," I said, trying to sound firm. "It's just not a good time right now."

"Okay," she said, sounding disappointed. "Maybe for the holidays?"

"Sure," I said. "That sounds great. Let's plan on it."

It didn't feel like small talk. With Holly it never does. We tiptoe around the edges a little, but we can also dive into the well when we need to.

"I was going through some old photos," I told her, ready to change the subject. "There's a great one of you sitting on the hood of our old Impala. Showing off your legs, as usual."

She snort-laughed. "Do you remember when we got picked up by the sheriff after I first started driving, and we never let Mama know?" she said.

"Yeah," I laughed. "We were so afraid he was going to call her, we wouldn't let her answer the phone for a month after that."

"And the time we went on a double date and you ended up making out with Jason Leech?"

"And you abandoned me?"

"Hey, I couldn't help it if my date was a drag."

"Life has had a lot of ups and downs, hasn't it?" she said.

"Definitely," I said. And then, before we hung up, "I love you, sis."

DAY FIVE

I spent the day in the basement, the coolest place in the house, experiencing a sense of urgency to cross a few things off my list. I feel better knowing my lab results are in process. Now I just need to keep my mind off them until they arrive. Easier said than done.

As I walked into the cedar closet, I could hear Mama's voice as though she were right beside me. "Those old clothes aren't going to sort themselves." By noon, I'd filled five huge trash bags with wool jackets and shoes that went out of style years ago. I dragged them up the stairs and set them by the back door. *Maybe tomorrow I'll make a trip to Goodwill.*

I have so much to do; I certainly didn't expect to be entertaining company. But it turned out that I got together with Miriam Webster tonight. I've known that girl her whole life, and I still can't get over her name. I also can't get over the fact that I still think of her as a girl when she's forty-five years old. I babysat for her so often, I can't help picturing her at six years old with curly blond hair and a holster with cap guns.

Miriam always seemed like such an old-fashioned name.

And when she was in high school and started dating Rick Webster, I thought, *Holy cow, what if they get married?* I could just hear the jokes. *"There goes Miriam Webster, the walking dictionary."*

She's smart enough to be one, which is why it's always a pleasure to see her. She called about five o'clock this afternoon—an unexpected surprise. The power had gone out at four. Poof, just out. No lightning or thunderstorm, of course. There's still no rain in the forecast. I was in the basement, and all of a sudden I heard the sound of everything shutting down. I always think the house is completely quiet—but then I hear that awful dying down of the computer and the air-conditioning, and I realize how much I've been tuning out.

I did all the crazy things you do when the power goes out. I went into the kitchen and automatically reached for the light switch. I tried to turn on the TV to check for any news. Then I called the power company to report the outage, got an automated message, and realized I could be in for a long, hot night. I checked the thermometer outside the kitchen door: 107 degrees in the shade. I thought about making iced tea and got ready to put some water in the microwave to heat. Duh.

Then Miriam called.

She wanted to get together for supper since she was home alone, but she called the Mexican restaurant in town and they had no power, either. So she came over with chicken salad and margarita mix.

"Honey, I'm home!" she said when she showed up at the kitchen door. That's Miriam for you. She knocked, then let herself in, set the bags of food on the table, and tore a paper towel off the rack next to the sink so she could wipe the sweat off her forehead.

"I lost five pounds just walking in from the Jeep!" she said. "I'd hug you, but I don't think you want any of this."

She pulled at the front of her T-shirt and waved it back and forth to fan the perspiration.

"You're right," I said, setting out plates and glasses. "Between the humidity and my hot flashes, I have enough of that for both of us."

"What's this all about?" she asked, nodding toward the bags and boxes by the door while she opened the margarita mix.

"Oh," I said. "Just a little spring cleaning."

"In August?" she said.

"I'm either really late or really early," I said as I opened the freezer door for ice and let the wave of cool air flow over us.

We spread out the food on the kitchen table, moving like sloths so we wouldn't stir up any more heat. I hadn't seen Miriam since I had my last haircut at her salon, so she caught me up on her life.

Rick is coming back from his deployment for two weeks in October. The twins are already at school, helping with their pledge classes for their fraternity and sorority. Miriam joined a knitting circle but only went for a couple of weeks. "I love all those older ladies," she said. "I'm just not ready to be one."

After we ate, we took our drinks out to the porch to catch the slightest hint of a breeze. Miriam still has wavy blond hair, though she's added some honey-colored highlights. "I'm *way* too young to let the gray show," she always says. And I've got my curly red mop, which is only manageable thanks to her skills with the scissors. We both gathered our hair and held it up out of the way, pressing our cold glasses against our necks.

"Your freckles sure have faded," Miriam said. She stood up, came over behind my chair, and started arranging my hair in a high ponytail.

I stiffened and tried to shrug it off. But she was right. I hadn't even noticed.

"Dreadlocks," I said to change the subject.

"What?" Miriam asked.

"How would I look in dreads?" I asked, knowing how ridiculous the question was. "Two of the Lincoln cheerleaders came into the shop the other day, and one had dreadlocks. It got me thinking."

"Oh, honey," Miriam said, as though I'd given her a shot of caffeine. "Don't get me started. I've always wanted to do something different with your hair, but I never thought you'd be up for it."

She piled my hair up on top of my head, then let it fall down over my shoulders and ran her fingers through it to plump up the ringlets. "Next time you're in the shop, we're going to have some fun with it."

Next time? I thought.

I took a sip of my margarita. "How much time do you think you've spent in your life thinking about your hair, playing with it, styling it, wishing it were different?" I asked.

Miriam thought for a moment, then said, "Probably a solid two years of my life."

"Me too," I said. "Growing up, I always hated my ringlets. One time Mama threatened to shave my head if I complained about my hair one more time. 'Other girls spend a fortune on perms,' she said. 'Be grateful for what God gave you.'"

"Did you stop complaining?" Miriam asked.

"Are you kidding?" I said.

We both fanned ourselves with our napkins, which did us no good at all.

"Why does hair matter so much?" I asked her.

"I don't know," she said. "Look at us. I'm married to a man who could be shot or blown up at any moment.

You've lost your daughter and your mom. Maybe what we both need is some distraction. More fun, you know?"

She sat back down on the porch swing.

"Speaking of which," she said, "is there anyone special in your life right now?"

I always dread this question, and especially now. What could I say? That I feel no desire? That no one will ever replace Joe? That the thought of awkward conversation and a date at a coffee shop makes me tired? That a relationship means sex, and the idea does nothing to ignite the pilot light that flickered out a few years ago?

Or—oh—that I might be dead in another fifteen days?

"No," I said, "I stay busy just trying to keep up with things around here."

We were quiet for a few moments, listening to the cicadas and watching the moon rise. Despite the humidity in the air, it shone sharp and clear.

Out of the blue, Miriam asked me, "Meggie, would you mind if I told you something?" My heart sank, because I knew it wouldn't be good.

"No, I wouldn't mind," I said. "You know you can tell me anything."

She fell quiet again, and then she said, "I haven't said this to anyone, but I know I can trust you." How many times in my life have people said that to me and then revealed something so secret and deep that it takes my breath away?

"What is it, sweetie?" I said.

"I slept with someone last spring."

Oh my God. Rick was overseas facing IEDs and snipers, and Miriam was in bed with someone else.

"Oh," I said, my standard response when people tell me their secrets. Uncomfortable but trying not to show it. Trying not to judge.

"I can't believe I did it," she said. "And I only did it once. But we met at a party, and we both had too much to drink. I know how stupid that sounds . . . like something a twenty-year-old would say, not a grown woman with twenty-year-olds of her own."

"Have you seen him again?"

"No," Miriam said. The moon lit up her face, as if she was a little girl dreaming of what's beyond this universe of ours. "I don't intend to ever see him again. It wasn't an affair. Just one night of complete stupidity. I adore Rick. I just miss being with a man, you know?"

"Are you going to tell him?" I said.

"What do you think? Should I? That's why I wanted to tell you . . . to get your advice. You always know the right thing to do."

I drew in a deep breath at the irony. In the darkness, I shook my head. "Keep it between yourself and the moon," I said. "It would do no good for Rick to know. But you've got to let go of it. If you keep carrying it with you, it'll eventually break you down and things will never be the same with Rick and he won't know why."

"But how do I do that?" she said. I saw the tears on her cheeks in the moonlight. "How do I let go of it? I've never done something unforgivable before. Crazy and unfair and hormonal and uncalled for, yes," she said, wiping the tears from her cheeks. "But not out-and-out unforgivable."

Who am I to give her any advice on forgiveness? I thought. *How can I tell her to do something I think is impossible?*

"I think that one's between you and God," I said. "It's never made sense to me that He would make us human and then judge us for being human," I said. I pushed the porch swing back and forth with my legs. "You make things right with yourself," I said, "and I'm pretty sure God will be on board."

We were quiet again; the only sound was the creak of the porch swing.

"So, how about you?" Miriam said. "Do you have any secrets you want to share?"

I stopped swinging and tried not to be too transparent.

"No," I said, moving the swing again. "I haven't had a secret for years."

No matter how much we fanned ourselves, sweat trickled down our faces and ran down our necks. Miriam slipped off her top and dropped it to the porch beside her, then stretched out the front of her bra and fanned air between her breasts.

"Great idea," I said and did the same. It felt good to spend time with someone who wasn't judging me, either for my cellulite and stretch marks or my decision to live or die.

Along about ten thirty, the power finally came back on. I heard the hum of the refrigerator, the blessed air-conditioning fan kick in.

Miriam and I looked at each other and said, "Thank God!" at the same time. We ran in the house to stand in front of the vents while the cool air flowed over us and dried up the sweat and tears. We held our hair out of the way to feel the cool air on our necks.

Miriam's eyes were bright green in the light, and she smiled as she looked at me.

"What would someone think if they walked in right now and saw us both in our underwear?" Miriam asked.

"They'd think, 'Damn, those lesbians look good,'" I said.

When Mama passed away, I decided to stay in the house. It's where I grew up, and it has always been home. Even when Joe and I had our own place, even when Rose was little, we still wanted to be here at Christmas. Mama always made turkey and trimmings for all of us, since Holly and her family only lived twenty minutes away back then.

And spending time with Joe's family wasn't an option. He walked away from his parents when he was seventeen and never looked back. That's one of the reasons why Mama adopted him like her own.

In a way, I felt relieved to give up the house I'd shared with Joe and Rose. And Mama was more comfortable here. She could still do some gardening when I first moved back, and I'd help her weed and we'd talk and laugh out in the garden.

"Do you still remember your dad at all?" she asked one day when we were deadheading the flowers.

"Sure I do," I said. I could tell that surprised and delighted her.

"What do you remember? You were so little when he died."

"I remember the time I locked myself in the bathroom and couldn't get out, and he had to come in through the window to get me."

Mama laughed.

"And I remember him taking us all to Henry's for hamburgers. What did they cost then? A quarter?"

"Probably," she said. "You were five years old before you'd eat an entire hamburger."

"That's right," I said. "I remember him saying, 'You don't eat enough to keep a bird alive.'"

"He was a good man," Mama said. "He was so proud of his girls."

I didn't want to ask the question, but something compelled me. "Do you ever wonder what your life would be like if he was still alive?"

"Of course I do," she said. "Even after all these years. We'd probably still live here, we'd fly out to see Holly and her family once a year, and we'd still have as much sex as ever."

I have to admit, I did not see that one coming.

*   *   *

Joe and I never thought Rose would grow up so fast. She expected a lot of herself and didn't like to make mistakes. She took special pride in spelling, which Mama said was a skill she inherited from her grandpa. When her class held a spelling bee, she came home close to tears and told us in a serious tone of voice that she'd misspelled *embarrassed* in front of the whole school.

"I knew better," she said. Joe sat with her at the kitchen table and looked her in the eye like she was an adult. She didn't flinch or look away, but held his gaze.

"You can't let mistakes stop you," he told her. "Don't give them any more than their due."

She nodded, taking in his words.

"Here's what you do with a mistake," he said. "You treat it like a mosquito bite. Instead of scratching and making it worse, you treat it, learn from it, and move on. Don't give it any more space in your life than that."

Rose nodded again, riveted.

"If you keep going back and reliving the mistake or second-guessing yourself, you'll never have peace," he said. "Your life will be devoted to mistakes rather than moving forward. And you're likely to keep making the same ones over and over."

He smiled at her. "Make sense?" he said.

"Yep," she said. "Thanks, Dad."

That was Joe. The rock we could count on. No wonder his offspring was the perfect balance of steadiness and wonder.

When Rose was four, she asked Joe, "Are your mom and dad dead?"

"No, Ladybug, my parents are alive," he said, just as matter-of-fact as she was. "But I haven't seen them for a long, long time."

"Why not?" she said. "Are you mad at them?"

"No, not really," Joe said. "But they were mad at each other and themselves, so I left home and never went back."

"Don't you miss them?"

"Sure I do. But I missed them even while I was living with them. Sometimes people just aren't themselves." He looked at her. "That probably doesn't make much sense, does it?"

"Yes, it does," Rose said. "Like how you miss Mommy when she's mad at you."

Once someone asked me what I would miss about my life if I died. It struck me as an odd question. It's a little like asking someone in solitary confinement what they'll miss when they finally get out into the sunshine. It's not that life is like solitary confinement, but I think what's on the other side is so remarkable that the last thing I'll do is be pining over my life.

But if you were to ask me what I've enjoyed most about my time here, I would say being a mom and a wife. After that, it would be planting flowers. So many times on mild April and May days, I felt a primal urge to get home, change into my gardening pants and shoes, and go dig in the dirt. I'd count the minutes until I could touch the soil, the way Rose used to count the days until we set out cookies for Santa Claus.

It's just remarkable to me how much life force there is in a tiny plant. How much it wants to grow. But then when fall comes, it's time to let go. The flowers know it. No matter how much you water or feed them even in a good year, they start to look peaked.

That's why I think this whole idea of keeping us alive until we're ninety and a hundred is not necessarily nature's way. I'd rather go before I have years of decline. But maybe

I'm just trying to rationalize the fact now that I have no choice. Well, maybe it would be more accurate to say I've made my choice. Funny—usually we say, "I've made my choice; now I'll have to live with it."

Not this time.

Fine. I never could tell a joke.

DAY SIX

I woke up in the middle of the night last night and heard the howl of coyotes. It sounded like they had congregated right outside my bedroom window—that horrible sound of marauders that have found their prey. I immediately thought of the kittens, four balls of fur that are just old enough to wander away from their mom. I opened the window and screamed at the coyotes, a wellspring of sadness and anger rising up in me.

I slept fitfully for the rest of the night. I shoved the sheets off me and pulled them back up, got up to turn the ceiling fan on higher and then turn it down.

Sometimes panic crawls over me, burning through me. I go to sleep without any trouble because I'm so exhausted, and sleep is so welcome. But when I wake up at three in the morning, the fear starts in my stomach and starts spreading through me like venom.

I wonder if that's what the pearls are doing. Are they working? What will my blood work show? I'm guessing the pearls were tested on soldiers, strong men who weighed much more than I do. And how did they test them anyway?

How did they know the pearls would take twenty days on a human? Who signed up for *that* experiment?

But I'm not in a place to judge, am I? I've noticed this more and more each day. As soon as I start to judge anything—even the weather for being so hot and dry—I feel the hands of something invisible pulling me back, like a stern but gentle parent sitting me down and saying, "Let's think this through." I can't judge anything anymore, except myself.

I look younger. My skin actually looks softer, more youthful. Maybe I'll have the benefits of the pearls without the final result. And every time I hope for that, another part of me thinks of how good it would feel to see Rose and Mama again, and I'm right back there at the kitchen table, stirring the green pearls into my yogurt and thinking I've made the right decision.

I spent the afternoon going through more boxes in the basement. I turned on the dehumidifier, put on my shorts and T-shirt, and went down with a broom to sweep away any cobwebs or mouse droppings or bugs as I got back into the corners that I haven't cleaned out for years.

Mama and I always kept most of the photo albums and papers in the bedroom closets, where they'd be protected from mold and bugs. But I found one box in a corner of the furnace room. Why it got overlooked, I don't know. Maybe I never saw it, and Mama wanted to forget it.

At first I thought I'd pitch it all—tax records from twenty years ago, a ledger Mama kept of the furniture she repaired and sold. Historic, but not very personal. But underneath those was a snapshot. Black and white, like they were in those days, with wavy edges and a date stamp in the margin.

It's a picture of Holly and me taken about six months after Daddy died. In the photo, we're wearing matching dresses with plaid bodices and khaki skirts, and both of us have bangs and curls. We're holding hands, and Holly is clutching her first Barbie to her chest. I have two front teeth missing. We look adorable and desperate at the same time. Seeing that photo is like looking at our roots, like the seeds of who we are and were to become.

It made me sad to see the photo buried, as though it had been in a grave all these years. It deserved to be resurrected. I went upstairs, called Schwan's Drug to see if they could copy and enlarge it, and added it to my to-do list for tomorrow.

I know all of these things will be Holly's in a few days anyway, but the photo made me realize how much I need to see her after all. If I don't do it before August 28, I'll carry regrets with me on that final day. And of all the things I want to clean out and let go of, regrets are at the top of the list.

I want to deliver this photo to her in person. So I texted her before I could talk myself out of it.

Hope the offer still stands for me to come see you. Booking a flight. Okay to come Thursday?

Thirty seconds later, she texted back.

Can't wait! Your room is ready. Send me your arrival time and I'll be there.

I took several deep breaths and leaned against the refrigerator to steady myself. What had I just committed to? And simultaneously, how could I have gone so long without seeing my family?

With my trip to Holly's, I'll have to work faster to stay on schedule. But that's okay. The pile of To Donate bags and boxes by the back door is growing, so I'm making progress.

And I've noticed something unexpected about cleaning things out: The more I let go of, the lighter I become.

Still, it's painful to do the deep cleaning. No wonder I've

put it off. With every box I open, I wonder what memory I'm going to face next. I needed an ultimate deadline to force me over the threshold of fear.

But I found something today that made me smile. Christmas cards. Grouped together by year and stored in big mailing envelopes, bound by ancient rubber bands that broke when I pulled out the cards.

I sat back on the chair I always meant to paint and started reading them. Notes from old family friends, from Mama's one brother who died young. From parents of my classmates and Holly's, from folks at church. And from my adult life, too. Friends of Joe's and mine. I forgot how we used to keep these. A bigger community than I remembered. So many people I lost touch with after Mama died and I folded myself inward.

I also found a stash of blank, mismatched, leftover envelopes that somehow got separated from their greeting cards—a testament to Mama's thrift. So I have discovered the way to resume communication and say good-bye at the same time.

I'm finding a card from the people I remember and appreciate most and am sending it back to them with a note of thanks. The middle of August seems like an odd time to send Christmas trees and reindeer through the mail, but there are angels, too. And they belong any time of year.

Rose always seemed like a grown woman in some ways. She sat with her back straight and seemed to get all the little girl giggles out of her by the age of three. After that, she bounced and skipped with delight, but she took life seriously. I wonder sometimes if she knew hers would be short, and she was trying to squeeze in all that she could. At the most unexpected times—waiting in line at the grocery store or vacuuming out the car—memories have popped up out of nowhere, and I've wondered what adventures she would have had. How she would have surprised us.

When I was sixteen, Mama and I went to the store to buy a new dress for Homecoming, and we ran into some friends she hadn't seen for a long time—ones I'd never met. We were standing outside Miller's Hardware Store and next to the fabric shop, where we bought the lengths of polyester and cotton for most of my clothes.

It was a treat to be buying a ready-made dress, especially one for my first real date. I'd hung out with boys in groups before, but my first one-on-one called for something special. I envisioned a dress with a fitted bodice and a flared skirt in light blue—the right color to show off the navy-and-white school colors corsage I was sure Frank Foster would give me.

I'd never seen Mama look the way she did when she spotted the Evanses. She squared her shoulders and tucked in her chin, like a turtle pulling into her shell.

"Why, how are you?" she said, shaking hands with them both. Her formality took me by surprise, since she typically greeted old friends with an all-out hug.

"Real good, real good," they said, bobbing their heads up and down. Mr. Evans wore a long coat, and Mrs. Evans actually wore white gloves—a throwback to another time, since bell-bottoms and halter tops had long since taken over. It was odd to see both styles on the street, as though we lived on two planets simultaneously.

"I haven't seen you for years," Mama said. Her voice sounded like she wanted to be cordial and warm, but I could tell she forced herself to say the words with any emotion.

"We're just back in town for a visit," Mrs. Evans said. "We're on our way across the country and thought we'd come see our old stomping grounds."

I knew my mother. I could feel her inner conflict. Typically, this was the point when she'd say, "Well, for heaven's sake, come by our place for a cup of coffee. We need to catch up after all these years."

I'd heard Mama do it a hundred times. She invited people into her home and her life like she was bringing new flowers into the garden. And people always came. I never had that skill, being more of a loner. But when I was little, it was not unusual to have two or three people stop by every Sunday, lingering over a piece of coconut cake and a bottomless cup of coffee. Holly and I sat in the living room, playing with dolls and eavesdropping on every conversation.

But this time, Mama didn't say those words. I could feel they were stuck in her throat, that she was willing herself *not* to say them. She didn't know how to finish a conversation without issuing an invitation, though, so it felt awkward. A pained silence.

"Well, it's good to see you, Lillian," the couple said again. And they walked on down the street, arm in arm.

"Who were they?" I whispered as we walked away. I took Mama's arm to steady her.

"That was Ruth," she said. "She was my best friend at one time. And her husband is Ralph—the man I almost married."

Something in her voice told me not to ask. Part of my mother's life had been a secret, and she wanted to keep it that way. She'd never mentioned a Ruth or a Ralph. They didn't exist in her photo albums or scrapbooks, which I'd pored over on rainy afternoons dozens of times.

That was when I started seeing her as a human being as well as my mom, and it was the first time I realized that we live many lifetimes within one life. Sometimes we pack up events and relationships and put them on the shelf, pushing them toward the back and closing the door on them.

I wonder if that's why it's so hard to sort through old stuff, especially the reminders of life cut short. It means confronting the memories, uncovering something we've mercifully forgotten that can wield power over us in an instant.

After Rose died and Joe left, I started volunteering at the children's hospital to pay penance, I think, as an act of contrition. Maybe if I helped enough kids, I could wake up in the morning without being disappointed I hadn't died in the night. But how many would be enough? How many kids would it take to atone for losing Rose and Joe?

Now I can see why the kids in the hospital were always so honest. What else *is* there when you know pretending doesn't matter anymore?

One little boy named Stuart made the most lasting impression on me. He had cancer and had lost his hair. Every day he played with the same toy, a NASCAR matchbox car. He was about seven years old. I asked him if he'd ever been to a NASCAR race.

"Me and my dad went last year," he said. I sat on the edge of his bed and leaned over to hear him. Exhausted from the rounds of chemo and radiation, he took deep breaths between sentences. But he rolled that car over his sheets and his pillow, making *vroom, vroom* sounds to go along with it. He'd do that for several minutes at a time, then he'd lie back with his head on the pillow and hold the car in his hands, spinning the wheels, totally absorbed.

"I'm sorry I won't get to go to another race," he said to me. I had come in to pick up his tray and stayed to talk for a minute. I wanted to say something inane like, "What do you mean? You'll get to go to loads of races. You'll be up and around before you know it." But I'd learned with Rose that you don't lie to a dying child. They know what's happening, and they only want you to be honest.

So I said nothing.

"I hope my dad goes to the races whenever he wants," he said, "and I hope he doesn't feel sad that I'm not there with him. I don't want him to be lonely."

He said it so innocently and with so much compassion, as though he knew exactly how his dad would feel and wanted to spare him that pain. Did Rose know how lonely I'd be without her? Can kids have any idea how much their presence fills up their parents' heart, and how empty life seems without them?

I put my hand on his head for a moment, straightened his sheets, and asked if he wanted more ice cream. "No thank you," he said. Then he closed his eyes and looked so peaceful, like angels filled every corner of that room.

Two days later, I found out he'd passed on. I never met his parents, but I bet his dad carried that toy car in his pocket for years. And I prayed that he wasn't lonely.

Even as I said the prayers, though, I knew full well that this was one request even God couldn't grant.

I never met any of Joe's family. Not a one. The youngest of three boys, he grew up in a small town in Illinois, fascinated by building and fixing things. His dad spent most evenings and weekends at the Bon Ton on the corner, getting drunk with his buddies. One brother served time in prison, and the other worked as a mechanic. Unlike their father, he got drunk mostly at home.

Joe didn't fit his family. He saw that all of them were on a self-destructive path, and he couldn't save them. When he was seventeen, trying to defend his mom, he punched his dad in the face and broke his nose. His dad kicked him out of the house, and Joe never went back, divorcing himself from all of them.

With Joe's even temper, he understood his family's patterns from the time he could walk, and he decided not to be bitter. He just didn't want to be like them or with them.

He was direct, like Rose, but gentle about it. He never raised his voice. He just asked questions. It drove him crazy when I withdrew into myself and shut him out. Some men joke about liking the quiet treatment, but not Joe. He figured any problem could be solved if we just took it out and looked at it together. But I hid my feelings a lot and, in his view, came to conclusions that didn't take all the information into account. When I felt scared or angry or worried, I usually blamed myself, and I'd hide rather than looking at things in the light.

Joe never criticized me for that tendency, but he worked with Rose to make sure she could face down a problem and not be afraid of it; then he taught her the skills to figure things out. Some evenings, the scavenger hunts he set up for her led to a special prize. Maybe tickets to the amusement park or a new book on bugs.

He'd give her the first clue, which might lead to a bucket in our garage or the crook in her favorite tree. The next clue might take her to a flowerpot on the stoop or a hole in one of the railroad ties edging our flower beds. On and on she'd go, finding her way, not giving up, searching until she found the next clue. He'd go with her to help if she got way off course, but he let her figure out the clues and the next moves herself. And if she made a mistake, he didn't give her the right answer.

"I want her to be as capable as you are," Joe once told me. We were standing outside on a spring evening, watching Rose and Cricket running through the yard for the next clue.

"You think I'm capable?" I said. I wasn't fishing for compliments. I honestly didn't see myself that way.

"Of course," he said, surprised by my own doubts.

"You've always been there for your mom and Holly, and now for me and Rose. None of us would know what to do without you."

I leaned against him and put my arms around his waist.

"In fact," he said, "sometimes I think you worry about us too much. You can share those burdens with me, you know."

"I know," I said.

He was right, but I always had a hard time letting go.

Mama and I always got along pretty well, even during my teenage years. The angriest I ever saw her was the summer before my senior year in high school. She was scheduled to judge the flowers at the State Fair and was headed to town early. I'd been out with some friends the night before, and I neglected to get the beer bottles out of the car before Mama went to use it the next day.

She came roaring into my bedroom at seven a.m. like the wrath of God, holding a beer bottle in one hand and the car keys in the other.

"Were you drinking last night?" she yelled. I sat up in bed and cowered, afraid she was going to hit me. I'd never felt such anger from her before.

"No," I said. "The others were, but they had me drive."

"What do you mean, they were drinking?" she yelled. "None of you is old enough to drink. Let me smell your breath," she said, towering over me.

She leaned in to take a whiff, then backed off since there was no evidence, and I could see her shoulders slump.

"You know that train conductor was drunk," she said, as though we'd just been talking about Daddy and picked up in the middle of the conversation.

Mama never talked about the accident. I had no idea.

"No, Mama, I didn't," I said quietly.

"Well, you're going to tell me who you were out with, and I'll be on the phone with those parents," she said. I cringed. "And you're grounded until school starts."

Two weeks. I seethed for the rest of the day, snapping at Holly and holing up in my room all day to read and listen to music.

"What got into her, anyway?" I said to Holly when I came out of my room to fix a sandwich for lunch. "I've never seen her that mad."

She looked at me as if I'd turned green. "Really?" she said. "You don't think she might be just a little emotional about Daddy?"

"Well, how was I to know?" I said, putting up the jar of peanut butter. "She never told *me* about the train conductor. Did you know?"

"Nope, first I've heard of it," Holly said. "But beer bottles in the car? C'mon. You've got to admit, that was pretty stupid."

"Yeah," I said, "next time I'll stop at the Dumpster by Ted's Market on the way home."

And I did. Years later, when Joe and I were married and he helped Mama go through old financial records, I found out why she was so on edge that summer.

"Did you know your mom almost lost the acreage?" he said one day while he was browning sausage for breakfast.

"What?" I asked. "What do you mean?"

"Eight years ago," he said. "She was behind on property taxes, and the bank almost put the place into foreclosure."

"Are you kidding?" I said, gripping my coffee cup. "She never told us a thing about it."

"Well, I'm sure that doesn't surprise you," Joe said. "You know how independent she is. And she always wanted to protect you and Holly."

I thought back and remembered her mood around that

time. Fragile, emotional. Her reaction to the beer bottles was part of a larger pattern, but I'd been too caught up in my own adolescent angst to notice.

"What did she do?" I asked.

"Larry Willis helped her restructure the debt," Joe said. "And she sold the parcel of land at the back of the property to the Logans. That gave her enough cash to get up to date."

"That's why she sold it?" I sat back in my chair, remembering. "She told us she wanted to downsize since Holly and I would be going off to college, blah, blah, blah. She never let on about any financial trouble."

"Well, don't tell her I told you," he said, putting our breakfast dishes in the sink. "I'm supposed to keep these things in confidence, but I just thought you should know. In my experience, keeping secrets eventually takes its toll."

DAY SEVEN

This morning I woke up with a sense of purpose. Wound the clock. Fed the cats. I've only seen two of the kittens in the past couple of days, but I am determined not to worry.

Then I took care of one of the most urgent items on my "bucket list" and went to see Larry Willis to make some changes in my will. He's been our family lawyer for as long as I can remember. He set up a memorial fund for Rose. He handled my divorce and Mama's estate. She always used to say that he knew more of the intimate details about us than anyone outside the family.

I parked outside his office on the square and went in for our appointment the same as always. This time, though, I saw things I've never noticed before.

In the reception area, a TV was tuned to CNN. While I sat for a few minutes, I couldn't help but hear the news of the latest mass shooting. I felt that I'd been ripped out of slumber, seeing the event in a new way. For the first time I can remember, I felt no anger toward the shooter. Just a sense of peace that things will be okay. I couldn't explain it.

When I went into Larry's office, I saw his diplomas on

the wall. He graduated from Notre Dame. Did I ever know that? Surely I did somewhere along the way. But does he have two children or three? Are they still in college? Is he a grandpa? He must be by now, but I couldn't say for sure. Where have I been? Why don't I know these things about a man I've known my whole life, who has played such a big role in my family at the most significant times in our history?

He looked a little older, a little grayer than when I saw him last. "Something's different," I said as we sat down in his office. "Do you have a new pair of glasses?"

"Yes," he said, "the wife finally convinced me to update my frames. I don't know why." He smiled. "Every ten years or so is good enough for me. But apparently she wanted me to look a little more up-to-date in our son's wedding photos."

Ah, an answer to one question, anyway. Normally I would have glazed over it and gone on with our business. But I stopped this time.

"Is the wedding coming up?"

"No," he said, leaning back in his chair, clearly pleased to talk. He turned around and took a photo off the shelf behind him. "They got married in June. Traditional all the way."

I looked at the photo—really *looked*—where normally I'd give it a glance and go on.

His son looked just like him. Tall, dark hair, trim build, and softness around the eyes. He beamed next to his bride, a brunette in a strapless white gown who looked completely comfortable in her own skin.

"They're a beautiful couple," I said. "I'm embarrassed that I can't remember your son's name."

"Larry Junior," he said. More embarrassment.

"And his wife is Liz. They live in St. Paul . . . happy as clams."

"That's wonderful," I said. "I hope you get to see them as often as you like."

"Sure thing," he said, setting the photo back on the shelf. "Our family likes to get together. Anytime we can have a golf game and a barbecue, we've got an excuse to visit."

It sounded like a good life. Like all anyone would need.

"So," he said, "tell me how I can help you today."

"I'd like to make some changes to my will," I said. I surprised myself at how matter-of-fact I sounded, as though I was ordering ground beef at the butcher counter.

"All right," he said, taking a more businesslike tone. "I'd be happy to help." He looked me in the eye and said, "I have to ask, is there anything that's prompting you to make the change right now?"

He wanted to know if I was sick. If I was dying. It was my chance to say it out loud, to get it out in the open, to send up an SOS if I wanted.

"No, nothing in particular," I said. "It's just been on my mind lately, and I thought I'd get it taken care of."

"Certainly," he said, turning around to his computer. "Let me pull up your file."

Within half an hour, I reallocated my savings, including my inheritance from Mama, moving most of it from the children's hospital to the trust funds for Holly's kids. I'm glad Holly will get all the proceeds from the sale of the acreage. It's only fair, when I've been living there rent-free since Mama died. Holly said it was the least she could do to repay me for taking care of Mama, but now it's Holly's turn to reap some rewards. I know she and Phil are stressing about college tuition, so this will help ease the burden.

Larry printed out the amended will and had me sign it, and I gathered up my purse to leave. "So, everything is going okay for you, Meg?" he said. "You keep looking younger all the time. You must have a secret."

"Guess I just have good genes," I said.

* * *

When I got home, I tied my hair up with one of Mama's handkerchiefs, put on a tank top and old shorts, and started taking more boxes out of the shed. I want to get this cleaning done before I leave for Seattle.

In one of the boxes, I found the art supplies we bought when Rose was little. I can see her at age five in her jeans and T-shirt, that thick hair pulled back in a ponytail and one of my old aprons wrapped around her, practically chin to toe. We put an easel under the oak tree near the back door, where she'd paint for an hour at a time.

We couldn't believe her attention span at such a young age, but she barely moved, fully absorbed, painting pictures of the hills and the trees or our family. Her artwork always included bugs and bats crawling in the landscape or flying overhead.

I suppose a therapist might have read some dark meaning into that obsession, but critters were nothing but joy for her. She learned words like *centipede* and *arachnid* at an early age and could tell you exactly what they meant. The word *guano*, as in bat dung, was one of her favorites, and she said it with pure glee.

One day she skipped over to the class bully on the playground, looked him right in the eye, and said, "You're guano," then skipped away. I don't know if she got away with it because she seemed so innocent or because he didn't know she'd just compared him to a pile of manure.

It surprised me to find those paints and brushes in the shed. I'm not sure why I kept them after Rose died. But there they were, right next to three shelves of paint cans. When I saw *those*, I suddenly felt tired.

For one thing, the heat made it hard to breathe. I opened the doors and hoped for a breeze, but the atmosphere felt just as oppressive. I got an extension cord and old box fan from the basement, but even that just stirred up the thick air.

I was determined not to quit, though, no matter how much energy it took to make a decision about every one of those cans.

As I picked them up and set them on the floor of the shed, I could tell most were half empty, and some were from our old house. I must have moved them to Mama's and stored them with hers. Joe and I painted many rooms over the years—Rose's nursery, our kitchen, every room inside Mama's house. Maybe it was time to paint again.

Well, that's silly, I thought. I don't need a fresh coat of paint on the walls now.

I read the names of the colors on the labels: Teakwood Brown. Nut Butter. Cotton Candy. Golden Delicious.

Mama might not have had a man around to keep everything in good repair, but her store of paint helped her keep it all looking fresh and trim. She used to say, "Don't get sad, get busy."

As soon as she saw something looking dingy, she got out the brushes and stepladder and cleaned it up. She referred to paint as her fix-all. "You can spend five thousand dollars on remodeling or fifty dollars on paint, and you won't be able to tell the difference," she used to say.

That's why the kitchen cabinets dated back to the time before I was born, and the bathroom still had its original black-and-white tile on the floor.

"See?" Mama would say, pushing the latest *Better Homes and Gardens* under my nose. "The bathroom's back in style again."

"Yeah, for the third time," I'd say.

I lined up all the cans and looked at them, thinking how hard it would be to dispose of them properly. It would mean a trip to the recycling center either for me or Holly. So I picked up a screwdriver and started prying them open.

I found colors that reminded me of when I was a teenager and we painted signs for Mama's antiques business and put them out by the road.

And I found colors that surprised me—colors I hadn't ever seen used in the house. Bright shades of purple and teal, raspberry and lemon yellow. "Where did these come from?" I wondered. Maybe Mama had stored them for friends who forgot them. Maybe she bought them for furniture she never got around to. Maybe she thought I'd use them someday.

Some just had a quarter inch of dried-out paint at the bottom, cracked and flaking, but others were almost full. I found the lavender we used for the nursery the first time I got pregnant. The color stayed with us through all the miscarriages and Rose.

I opened up the soft greens and tans of the living room and kitchen. The bright fuchsia I used in a misguided moment in the bathroom.

Some had been sitting so long that they were white when I looked in the tranquil pool of the bucket. As I stirred, I watched the colors come to life before my eyes. One showed a faint hint of orange before morphing into a vibrant coral. Another seemed iron gray until cornflower blue emerged.

The stirring put me into a reverie, and I had an experience that has been occurring more often lately.

Doing something totally mundane turns into a feeling I can't describe. Harmony, maybe. I actually felt myself *with* the paint instead of thinking about five other things at the same time. It was as though I've lived my whole life through a Plexiglas shield or a plastic bag, everything buffered and filtered and muffled through some layer of fear. And now I felt present, engaged. Alive.

Then, all of a sudden, a pesky fly jolted me back.

It's too damn hot out here, I thought, especially when another hot flash hit and I wanted to jump out of my body.

I carried a few paint cans into the house where I could look at them in the air-conditioning and figure out what to do. I lined them up on the kitchen table and thought back to the time when Holly and I were little and we drew on the wall.

Mama didn't scold us. She stood back, looked at our artwork, said we were budding Picassos, then bought us an easel and big pads of paper.

Something came over me, as if I was seven years old again. I looked at the kitchen wall, and for the first time saw it as it could be. Without hesitation, I took the pictures down and piled them in the living room. Then I set the hanging spice cabinet on the counter, and I pulled the table and chairs out from the wall.

No clock. No towel rack. No knickknacks. Just a blank canvas, beckoning me.

I picked up a paintbrush, dipped it in a can of apple green, and drew it across the wall in a wide swooping arc, almost from one end to the other.

Abandon. Play. No neat lines, no defined spaces. Just one big easel and permission to fill it with whatever I wanted. I opened another paint can and another and brushed colors on the wall wherever they wanted to go.

It felt deliciously illegal, as though I was breaking all my own codes of coloring within the lines.

I dipped the brush in the paint again and made another swirl. It felt so freeing, as though the motion unlocked a door I hadn't gone through in a long time. So I opened another can, teal this time, and got another brush and put more swirls on the wall. After fifteen minutes, I stepped back to look at the wall and literally gasped at what I saw.

I've started something. I don't know what. But it's my colored lights, the swirls of comfort I've missed since I was seven. Here they are, for real now, for everyone to see.

* * *

Rose would have been a wonderful big sister. After my last miscarriage—the one when she was two years old—Joe and I finally realized that Rose was more than enough, and we quit trying. But I gave thanks when Holly's boys were born and the three of them could play. Holly and Phil hadn't moved to Seattle yet, and they lived just twenty minutes away. So we got together whenever we could.

I remember when Rose was eight years old and the boys were four and thirteen months. We all went to the State Fair to watch Mama judge the flower show. Actually we just made a brief appearance. No matter how much the kids loved Grandma, they could only sit still so long while she sorted out the best coreopsis and coneflowers. When they'd had enough, we moved on to the livestock barns.

Rose shepherded the boys through the barns of goats and pigs as if she was their mom. She pushed Brent in his stroller and warned Mark when he stuck his hand in the pen with the giant boar. She sounded a lot like Mama, actually. "Now, Markie," she'd say, "be careful. That boar is way bigger than you are, and you're going to need those hands of yours to do great things when you grow up."

The boys clung to her. They'd do anything she said. One time when we were all at Mama's for the day, she even talked them into sitting still and letting her put spiders on their noses. I can just imagine what she said to them.

"It'll tickle at first." I'm sure she used her soothing voice, sounding like a master hypnotist. "But in a few seconds, you won't even know it's there."

When the boys walked into the kitchen with spiders crawling across their cheeks, Rose bragged about their courage, even though we all agreed it wasn't a good idea. That's how much confidence and trust she instilled in others. Lord only knows what she might have done with it.

*   *   *

I was admiring my kitchen artwork when the phone rang. It sounded muffled and faint. *Probably in my purse,* I thought, and went to retrieve it. I didn't recognize the number, but when I said hello, there was no mistaking the voice.

"Hi, Meg, how are you?"

I sat still for a moment, trying to orient myself to the sound.

"Joe," I said. "I'm fine. This is a surprise." I pulled out a chair and sat, staring at the swirls in front of me.

"Did you get my card?"

"I did, thank you. It was so nice of you to remember." I scratched at a spot of dried paint on my shorts, then looked back at the wall of color, trying to ignore the same butterflies I'd felt when I saw him at Mama's funeral.

"This must be a tough time for you."

"I'm getting through it," I said. "How are you?"

"Good. Everything's good. Say, I wanted to let you know, I'm coming to Iowa next week for a conference, and I'd like to get together and say hi."

He sounded casual, as though we did this all the time.

I thought for a moment. "Sure," I said, "it would be good to see you again. I'm headed to Seattle on Thursday, back on Sunday. Can we get together after that?"

"Oh," he said. "You'll be seeing Holly?" He sounded concerned.

"Of course," I said. "Just thought it was time for a visit."

"Good," he said. "You'll have to tell her hi for me. How about Tuesday?"

I looked at my calendar with the big red circle and the seven days I've marked off with red Xs. It's so odd to be booking appointments this way.

Day fifteen, I thought. "Sure, that would work. Want me to meet you in town?"

"That sounds good," he said. "I'll give you a call when you get back to set up the details."

Perfect, I thought after I hung up. I'd made a list of the people I needed to connect with, and he was on it. How nice that the universe brought him to me. *Life can be easy when you let it,* I thought.

When I went back to painting, I tried to put thoughts of Joe and the future out of my mind. *Who cares what the lab tests will show?* I told myself.

I got goofy, like I was punch-drunk, and danced while I painted. I made big swipes and curlicues in the air, humming to myself and hopping on one foot and then the other, splashing paint on the wall and then smoothing it in big arcs and spirals. I felt freer than I've felt in a long time, like when Holly and I used to dance to the *West Side Story* sound track when we were little.

I asked myself, "WWJRD—What would Joan Rivers do?" She'd say, "*Gawd,* after I die, I'll never have to wear a bra again." No more hot flashes and migraine headaches. No more belly fat or diarrhea or worrying about being a burden in my old age. No more shaving my legs—or not having enough hair to shave. No more cleaning the refrigerator, taking out the trash, paying bills, and worrying about rain.

And no more death. The ultimate irony. Dying means the end of death. I don't know for sure what it's going to be like on the other side, but I'm pretty sure flowers aren't going to wither and gasp in the heat. Kittens aren't going to be carried away by coyotes in the middle of the night. People aren't going to be bullying and murdering each other and plotting new, senseless ways to make other people suffer.

"I will not miss this place," I said over and over, like a mantra, as I painted. "I will not miss violence and ingrown toenails. I will not miss rude clerks at the grocery store and people who cut you off on the freeway. I will not miss famine and greed and hate. I will not miss crazy politicians and all of society's stupid rules. I'm going to a better place, and I will not miss this."

Then I sank into a heap on the floor and cried, because I hadn't convinced myself at all. No matter how much I try to ignore it, everything keeps getting more beautiful.

DAY EIGHT

I used to have dreams that I sold this acreage and moved into the city, into a little house in a marginal neighborhood. In the dream, I'd start to panic, wondering why I'd given up a home I loved so much and traded it for one I didn't. The sense of panic in the dream felt so real—the finality of something I couldn't undo. There was no going back, and the enormity of my regret knocked me flat.

That's how I feel. I never thought I'd have regrets when I took the pearls, even though I wasn't certain. But taking them has woken me up. I feel like I've emerged from some darkness, like I'm on a train that's nearing the end of the tunnel, and I want to get off the train and run out into the light before it crashes into the mountainside.

When I brushed my teeth this morning, I looked in the mirror and saw that the mole over my lip was gone. Just like that. No fading away gradually, no shrinking into nothing. Just gone.

I would have expected to rejoice for two reasons: First, I've always hated that thing. And second, it means the pearls are working. Isn't this the proof I wanted?

That's why my reaction startled me.

I was angry. All I've done the last few days is tell myself a bunch of lies about how happy I am to be going. Complete bull. I've been pretending, and on some level I've known it. I guess it wouldn't have been a lie otherwise.

This means the stuff is working. It means I have less than two weeks. It means I'm really leaving, and I'm not sure I'm ready after all.

The mole is gone, and there's no one I can tell, nothing anyone can do about it. Just like with Rose and my mom, there's no fixing it. But I am, by God, not ready to accept it after all, and I'm so angry at myself, I walked out on the front porch and screamed. That's the worst of it. I can't blame it on anyone, not even on God. With Rose, I could blame Him. But this was completely my choice, my decision.

I screamed and cried like I did days after Joe left—great, hacking sobs that rocked me back and forth.

So here's the honest truth: I'm scared to death.

No pun intended.

I've decided that if I have less than two weeks left, I'm going to experience life with as much joy as I can. And then it hit me: Maybe I could have lived this way without taking the pearls.

I never got the little green pearls out of the back of the freezer for Mama because she went downhill quickly at the end, and I knew the pearls wouldn't be necessary. For so long her physical health remained strong, but her mind kept shutting doors, and she'd often say, "I want to go home."

"But, Mama, you *are* home," I'd say. It helped knowing she was in a place she loved, even if she wasn't aware of it. "This is where you and Daddy lived your whole married life."

In her final year, she declined slowly and steadily. One

thing after another. Neuropathy in her foot. Arthritis pain. Difficulty swallowing. A hard time sleeping. Getting more and more forgetful. Holly came out from Seattle for a week every couple of months to help, and we had some money for a home health aide to come when needed. But Mama didn't want to go into a nursing home, and we didn't want that for her, either.

"I know how much pleasure she gets just sitting on the porch and looking out at the flowers," I told Holly. "If we took that away from her, I don't think she'd last another week."

"Sometimes I wonder if that wouldn't be better," Holly said. "I mean, is it even humane for her to go through this?"

That comment surprised me. I thought about what Dr. Edelman said when he gave me the bottle of pearls. It eased my mind, thinking Holly would probably agree with me if I ever decided to use them. I would have told her about it if things had ever gotten to that stage. But since they didn't, I couldn't see the point of having that conversation. Knowing that a white bottle with the number 20 on it sat in the back of the freezer gave me comfort yet haunted me at the same time.

Then one day Mama tried to get out of bed and fell and hurt her hip, and after that she was never the same. In those final days, I found great comfort in sitting with her. I couldn't wait to leave the shop; walk through the kitchen door; thank Sarah, the home aide; and sit with Mama, often in silence. People who are actively dying have given up trying and doing and are just being, and there's so much peace in it. No resistance. Just letting time ebb and flow over you like a shell on the sand, gently being washed out to sea.

On her last day, I tried to give her morphine to keep up with the pain, the way the hospice nurse showed me, but it just wasn't enough. I could see the end coming, though, and there was no need—or enough time—for the pearls. She tossed and turned as though she couldn't get comfortable. I called Holly and cried with her on the phone. Holly and her family had visited a month before, saying their good-byes before they left. But she kept me company on the phone that day.

Finally, late in the afternoon, Mama settled down. Her drawn face looked smooth and peaceful. She turned her head, reached out and held my hand, and looked right in my eyes. "I think I'll go to sleep now," she said, just as clear as could be.

I went to the kitchen just for a minute to get a glass of water. As I filled my glass, the ice made a tinkling sound just like her laugh when I was little. Then I felt nothing but stillness. "Mama," I said out loud. When I got back to her room, she was gone.

After she died, I stroked her feet, tied up her hair in a bun, and sat with her. I had the same sacred moment I'd experienced with Rose. The same sense of leaving, of unreasonable joy as the veil lifted for an instant and I could feel the world that welcomed my daughter, and now my mother, with open arms.

I missed that world, I realized. It felt like a place I longed for without even knowing it.

The next day, I sat on the sofa with Mama's afghan wrapped around me, and I felt her near me.

"I'm so sorry, Mama," I said. "I know you were in pain yesterday. I didn't know what to do to make it better."

"Don't give it a moment's thought," I heard her say. "You gave me everything I needed. No one could have done more."

I've started paying attention to every ache and pain. A twitch just below my eye. Muscle cramp in my foot. Feeling slightly nauseous or dizzy. I wonder if it's the pearls. Maybe I'm being punished for taking them. Or punishing myself for it. I know I've been crucifying myself ever since Rose died and Joe left.

I tried to talk myself down from my panic. Anyone could die at any moment. I could fall off the ladder and lie here by myself for days before Holly would send the police to find me. Or I could cut myself on the barbed wire fence and get lockjaw and die a slow and miserable death.

I tried to make light of the pearls. Will I wake up tomorrow and have a goatee? Maybe I could hurt myself enough that I'd need to go to the emergency room, and the doctors could give me something that would interrupt the action of the pearls and change the course of events. But I'm still not sure if I want the course of events changed.

Apparently I'm still searching for something and I don't know what. But I know if I'm going to find it, I'd better do it soon.

People say that memories of disaster are like a blur, but I experienced the opposite. Every moment of Rose's accident was seared into my brain in such great detail that, even now, thinking about it, my senses are fully engaged. Like the first time Joe kissed me or when Rose slid out of me with one heave of pain and ferocity. She was determined to come out whether I was ready or not.

That's how she did everything, with purpose and clarity. She was ten when she fell off Romeo, so she never reached that adolescent stage when girls' memory of who they are floats away in a sea of hormones and teen musicals. I sometimes wonder what it would have been like for Rose. Would she have lost herself? I would have done everything I could to help her retain her tenaciousness, her ability to size up people and claim her territory without offense. That capacity to comment on and guide people at the same time, while being genuine and holding her own ground.

She went with me the day I took Qasim to high school. Our church sponsored his family from Sudan, and Rose and I introduced him to his first day of school. Before the security officer would let us in, he asked for Qasim's ID, then he waved us through. Rose was just nine, but she recognized injustice when she saw it, and the officer's suspicion of black people caught her attention.

She stopped in front of the security officer, looked him in the eye, and said, "Why didn't you ask for *our* IDs?"

The officer didn't answer.

So here's what happened the day Rose had her accident.

It was June 25, and we'd come out to Mama's about two thirty in the afternoon. The daylilies and gaillardia were in bloom, the thermometer read 83 degrees, and the world seemed about as perfect as it could be. Joe was at work, I'd taken the afternoon off, and Rose and I stopped for ice cream on the way to Mama's and took her a chocolate milk shake.

I helped Rose saddle up Romeo like always, feeling the soft leather and rubbing Romeo's nose while he swatted flies with his tail. Rose wasn't an accomplished rider, but she'd been on Romeo since she turned six. His gentle nature and her levelheadedness made a good combination. In fact, Rose just rode around the pasture, never at a very fast clip, and Romeo patiently ambled along. I usually went back inside and helped Mama with some sewing, or we baked and caught up while the two of them had their outing.

This day we were baking a coconut cake when we heard Romeo snort and whinny, and then heard Rose scream. We'd just turned off the Mixmaster—otherwise we might have missed it. We ran outside and saw Romeo in the pasture, rearing up on his hind legs. We couldn't see Rose, and I knew what that meant.

As we ran toward Romeo, I kept expecting to see Rose pick herself up from the ground and brush herself off, take Romeo's reins, and stroke his nose. But Romeo stopped rearing and put his nose to the ground, so we knew exactly where to find her.

It was the perfect storm of unlikely possibilities. A snake at just the right place to spook the horse. A rock in the exact spot to crack her skull when her head hit the ground. Road construction on the highway that delayed the ambulance by several minutes.

Rose regained consciousness at the hospital and lingered for almost twenty-eight hours. But by seven o'clock that next night she was gone. Three days later, she was buried, the house was empty, and our life as we knew it was over.

Let me say something else about Rose. She was not a perfect child. When she was five, she took all the eggs out of their cartons and hid them in her closet so she could make cardboard caterpillars out of the boxes. When she was six and on a quest for candy, she sneaked Cricket into the grocery store, where he knocked over a display of cereal and then peed from all the commotion. When she was seven, she got into a fistfight with a boy in her class over an ice cream cone.

The time she got into the greatest trouble, she was eight years old and corrected her teacher, who misspelled *Pleistocene* in a unit about the Ice Age. Rose came home and complained to us. We were sympathetic but reminded her that she needed to show respect to her teacher.

Rose wasn't convinced and, instead of apologizing to Mrs. Conrad, told her that she wouldn't correct her again. She didn't seem upset when we grounded her for that.

But that's what I loved about her. Her ability to stand up for herself, to follow her imagination and her convictions.

She didn't see the colored lights as I did—at least she never said so. Not until the night she died.

Joe and I sat next to her bed, listening to the rhythmic sound of her breathing and heartbeat, amplified by the tubes and monitors. She'd talked to us earlier in the day but had been unconscious for two hours. Suddenly she stirred slightly, opened her eyes, and smiled.

We jumped up from our chairs and leaned over her, looking for some sign of hope.

But she didn't see us. She was looking at something beyond us, something only she could see. "They're beautiful," she said.

I recognized the softness and wonder in her eyes. I'd had that same look when I saw the swirls for the first time, all those years ago, not long before Daddy died.

I turned my head in the direction of her vision, wishing I could see what our little girl saw. It took just a moment, hardly a wisp of time. But when I turned back to look in my daughter's eyes, she was gone.

DAY NINE

I defrosted the refrigerator and chest freezer today. Two more things crossed off my to-do list. I piled all the frozen meals and packages of ground beef and chicken in our old Coleman cooler until I could put them back, then I sat down at the kitchen table with a glass of iced tea and looked at the empty freezer, imagining the bottle of pearls sitting there untouched for all those years.

Six years. And who knows how long Dr. Edelman had had them before that. They were decades old. Even if they had no expiration date, surely their potency would have waned a long time ago. For a moment, I convinced myself that they no longer had any power. That going to the doctor for lab tests was an overreaction.

But my freckles keep fading. And the mole I've had on my left arm since I was a girl is gone.

I can't go through any more photo albums. I might as well stick a knife in my eye or eat poison. And since I've already checked one of those off the list, I figure I've punished myself enough.

Three photos. That's all that put me over the edge. I pulled them out of their plastic sleeves in the albums and lined them up on the coffee table. I can't destroy them, even though looking at them may destroy me.

One is of Joe wearing Rose's ladybug mask after he took her out trick-or-treating when she was six. They were sitting at the kitchen table, candy spread out in front of them. Rose took off the mask because it itched, so Joe put it on. In the photo, he's crouched down over her chair, looking like he's going to steal a Snickers from the table. Cricket, wearing bug-like antennae, is giving him the evil eye. And Rose is sucking on a Tootsie Pop and looking up at her dad, giggling.

The second photo is from our wedding. We kept the guest list small since Joe didn't have any family coming. It's a picture of Mama, Holly, Joe, and me, taken in the garden out behind the church. The wind gusted on that June day, and my veil looks like it's about to take off and fly. Holly has Big Hair and an equally Big Bow at the waist of her tangerine dress, and Mama is looking regal in sage green. Joe has taken off his tuxedo coat and is reaching up to try to catch my veil. We're all laughing—one of the few snapshots I kept with all the formal portraits from that day.

The third one is of Mama two days before her fall. She's sitting on the couch with an afghan across her lap. The photo caught one of her more lucid moments, and she looks clear-eyed and focused, the way I remember her growing up. She's surrounded by plants. A bouquet of tulips and daffodils sits on the table next to her—one of the tables she repaired and antiqued with a gray stain at the height of her business days, then decided to adopt rather than selling it. A huge hanging basket with a blooming begonia is to the right, and a Norfolk Island Pine behind her looks as if it's growing out of her head and embracing her at the same time. I can't imagine a more fitting image to remember her by.

We had a routine during Mama's last months: I'd get up at five thirty, wind the clock, fix some eggs, feed the cats, do my list for the day, shower, and get dressed. Mama would wake up about eight thirty, and I'd have coffee ready for her. Sarah started her shift at eight thirty, so I'd say a quick good-bye to Mama and head out the door for work.

I came home at five thirty and said good-bye to Sarah, who started supper before she left. She usually fixed something simple—chicken with vegetables or a hamburger casserole. Mama and I sat down to eat at six. Then, if the weather cooperated, I walked with her around the yard, pointing out the flowers and trees.

"So pretty, so pretty," she'd say over and over. That was the hardest part of her decline. She went from being one of the best conversationalists I've ever known—interested in other people and generous with her own stories, a rare thing to find in balance—to being trapped within her own brain.

I've heard people describe folks with dementia as "child-like," but I never saw it that way. Children discover something new every day. Their vocabulary grows, and they find ways to communicate even when they don't have the words.

With dementia, it's a loss, not an addition. And when someone with Alzheimer's can't find the words, they don't know that there *is* a way, so they just clam up. Or they ask the same question over and over.

"Did you take the bacon out of the freezer?"

"Yes, Mama."

"Where is Eric's clock?"

"On the shelf, Mama."

"Don't forget to water the flowers."

"I won't, Mama."

I can only assume that every time she asked the same question, it was new to her. And every time I answered, that was new to her, too.

One day she woke up from a nap, came out to the kitchen in her robe and slippers, her long hair falling over her shoulders the way it did in the old photos of her as a girl. Mama's skin glowed, soft and unblemished, even after all those years in the sun.

"Is he home yet?" she asked. I assumed she was talking about Daddy but wasn't sure.

"Who do you mean, Mama?"

"Well, Ralph, of course," she said, a little peeved.

"Ralph?" I said, searching my memory bank. Did we have a relative named Ralph? Was he one of her customers? Then I remembered years before when we'd met Mama's former best friend and her husband, who had been Mama's fiancé.

"Ralph Evans?" I said, startled.

"Of course. Ralph," she said. "Where is he?"

"No, Mama," I said. "He's not back yet. Soon. I'm sure he'll be back soon."

Placated, she went back to her room and crawled into bed.

I put my breakfast dishes in the sink, a little shaken by her question. I figured she'd confused Mr. Evans with Daddy. It was understandable that in a mind affected by Alzheimer's, romance might take on other names and shapes, the loves of her life melding together into one memory instead of many.

Joe always cared a bit too much about organization, in my view, although he didn't cross the line into obsessiveness. And he never called me out for being messy, a trait my to-do lists never got under control. He always respected my needs, even when I stopped meeting his.

When we were first married and moved into our house down the road from Mama's, I carried bundles of clothes into the closets and hung them up until I ran out of room. It didn't matter to me if the shirts and skirts intermingled or my strappy sandals sat side by side with my winter boots. I just wanted to get the clothes in the house; then I'd sort them out someday.

Meanwhile Joe organized our books, CDs, and canned goods alphabetically. He kept them that way until the day he left.

Some nights while we watched TV, he spread out newspapers on the coffee table to keep it from getting scratched, then he dumped out his latest collection of miscellaneous screws and nuts, grouped them by size, and put them in recycled jars so they'd be easy to find.

He equipped his workbench with every kind of peanut butter and mayonnaise jar imaginable. Whenever we scraped out the last bit of strawberry jam or ate the last pickle, he soaked the jar in water, peeled off the label, dried it, and added it to his stash.

He had boxes of them in the garage, all on standby to hold machine parts, lightning bugs, coins, miniature gardens, spices, candles, and craft projects that he came up with for Rose. Her favorite was a snowman made from three jars of slightly different sizes. She and Joe filled them with cotton balls, stacked them, and glued them together, then painted a face on the top one and added a hat made from pipe cleaners and black felt. Rose kept that snowman on her dresser for years, replacing the cotton balls whenever the supply got low.

It's not that Joe was cheap. Far from it. He just liked the challenge of finding a new purpose for something that other people might throw away.

He also liked to prepare for eventualities. He paid the bills before they were due, kept several hundred dollars for emergencies in a pot Rose made in third grade, and winterized the house every fall.

Somehow the memory of all this made me think of one thing I hadn't yet prepared: my final wishes for a funeral.

I sat at the kitchen table with the laptop and started a folder called Meg's Last Wishes. I pulled my Living Will document into the folder, then wrote my instructions for a funeral.

If it were up to me, I started, *no one would wear black to my funeral. Children would release balloons, the more colorful, the better. And the only Bible passage would be the story of Jonah and the whale or Noah's ark. Not the 23rd Psalm.*

Please keep music light, a celebration. Nothing pious or maudlin. It's okay to play "I'll Never Find Another You," since we played it at Rose's and Mama's funerals. Flowers from Nancy's would be wonderful. And please direct any memorial contributions to the children's hospital foundation. Finally, I want to be cremated. Please scatter my ashes in the hills behind Mama's house, where I played as a girl with Holly, my sister and friend for life.

I printed it out, dated and signed it, and put a copy of it with my Living Will in the desk drawer so it would be easy to find.

Sometimes I look at the hills behind this house and am overcome by their beauty. Even in this scorching heat and without rain for the past seven weeks, the trees are green and lush when you look at the banks of them on the hillsides. Holly and I used to spend time wandering in those hills. We'd sit and wait for deer, and we learned to make a low huffing noise like the deer make. We could almost call them to us.

I loved this more than Holly did. She preferred Barbie dolls and makeup. But I could spend entire days outdoors wandering, climbing trees.

Rose took after me that way, but her connection to animals surpassed mine by far. You could see it in Romeo after her accident. He hung his head low, remorseful, as though he knew he'd played a role in her death. Rose asked me about him before she died. "Tell Romeo I don't blame him," she said to me. "He needs to know that."

This morning when I got up, humidity hung in the valley before the sun got bright enough to burn it off. It looked like clouds of steam, mystical, a shroud between two worlds. I wonder sometimes if the veil is truly that thin. If death is like stepping through that cloud of fog and seeing a shining hill on the other side.

I loaded up the car to take all the old clothes and housewares to Goodwill since I could hardly get past the stacks by the back door. And besides, it felt good to get them out of the house before leaving to see Holly. Fourteen bags and boxes altogether, stuffed with items that mattered once upon a time. But now that they're gone, I can't recall most of the contents of those bags. Funny how much meaning we give to things that will go away in the end.

On the way to Goodwill, I passed the church, of course. Since it's on the outskirts of town, I pass it every time I go anywhere. Most of the time I block it out, like the old stuff in the trash bags. But today the words on the sign caught my eye.

HURTING? WE'RE HERE FOR YOU, it said.

It reminded me of a church sign I saw once on the Internet: WE LOVE HURTING PEOPLE.

The memory made me laugh out loud. Sometimes what makes things funny is the truth embedded in them.

When I got home, I checked the mail, hoping the lab

results would be there. I figured if they showed any ab-
normalities, I could still cancel my trip and go in for more
tests. But they weren't there. Nothing but a credit card offer and two catalogs for clothes I won't be buying. So, a
few more days. Surely the results will be here by the time
I get back from Holly's. It may be too late, but very likely
it's too late already.

I called Miriam and asked if she'd come feed the cats
and water the gardens while I'm in Seattle. The timing
worked out well, since she's planning to spend a couple of
days with her kids, shopping for the rest of the stuff they
need at school. But she's not leaving until Sunday, the day
I get back.

"Don't stress about the gardens," I said. "No matter
how much water I give them, they still look parched and
tired at the end of the day."

The only thing keeping them alive is their deep roots,
and their ability to get what they need from moisture far
underground. The water I give them is nowhere near what
they need. In a typical year, with a steady supply of rain,
those roots would always have access to damp soil. Now,
with their stores depleted, they have to work harder for
every drop of nourishment. They plumb the depths, guided
by a life force beyond our understanding. I think sometimes about the secret subterranean world that keeps them
alive and give thanks for the nourishment we cannot see.

I need to see growing things. And I need to see my sister.

I asked Miriam to do one more thing. "I know it's kind
of silly," I said. "But would you mind winding the mantel
clock for me once each day? It belonged to Daddy, and I
just like to keep it running."

All I remember of Rose's funeral is sitting. I felt as if
my body couldn't support itself, and I'd already started to
lean away from Joe rather than toward him. He brought

me a chair so I could sit in the receiving line, hearing person after person struggle to find something comforting or meaningful to say. Most of the time, it came out wrong.

"At least she's with her grandpa now."

"You were wonderful parents. You can take comfort in that."

"Even though we don't understand, it must be God's will."

It seemed that people were speaking to me from underwater. Why wasn't anyone screaming at the top of their lungs? Why wasn't anyone shaking their fist at God? Why were we in a *church*, of all places?

We all went back to Mama's house and sat around the kitchen table, stunned and quiet. There were flowers everywhere. Memorial wreaths, bouquets, pots of schefflera and peace lilies. Their colors of hope seemed garish against the black we all wore.

Holly's boys were showing their fatigue. Mark went in the living room to watch a movie, and Brent, who was three, climbed into Holly's lap.

"Is baby sleeping?" he said, putting his hand on Holly's stomach.

I set down my iced tea and stared at Holly. "Baby?" I said. I saw Mama and Phil exchange concerned glances.

Holly's face went white. "We weren't going to tell you for a few more weeks. Until things settle down," she said.

I felt another blow to my stomach, as though I could feel her child kicking within me. And then I felt confused, disoriented, emotions all rising together into one volcanic cloud. I reached out for my sister's hand, too dizzy to get up and hug her.

"I'm happy for you, sis. I really am. That's wonderful news."

She squeezed my hand and said the one thing people in

all their clumsiness and discomfort had been trying to tell me all day. "I'm sorry," she said. "I'm so terribly sorry."

Joe stood behind me, his hands on my shoulders, and I felt his strength. Just a few days before, it meant everything to me. Now I could feel myself shrinking under his touch. Without Rose, everything was empty. My soul, my marriage—even the possibility of new life.

I leave for Seattle tomorrow. I'm excited and panicked at the same time. What will these days with Holly and her family bring? Then I'll come back and see Joe. Find out what my blood work shows. Part of me thinks I should cancel my trip and plant myself next to the mailbox until the lab results arrive. And then what? Regret missing my chance to see Holly? I can't win either way.

I took down my suitcase from the closet shelf, relieved to be leaving this heat behind for a few days. I packed sweaters and jeans, a shawl and a raincoat. A *raincoat*. Just think of that. And then I packed the photo of Holly and me, along with some keepsakes for the kids. But what will I say to her? I am determined to be joyful and honest. And yet there is this one piece of me, of my story, that I don't know if I'm ready to share.

What would be easiest for *her*? To know my decision ahead of time? To worry about what I've done? Or to believe that I peacefully passed in my sleep? To think, *At least we had these last few days together*. If I'm going to be in eternal peace, I want her to be, too.

DAY TEN

When I headed to the airport this morning, I had that same strange sensation I've been experiencing more and more each day. It's a little like when I got glasses in fifth grade. There I was, age ten, riding home from the appointment with the ophthalmologist. I sat in the backseat and looked at the trees going by and marveled that I could see each individual leaf. Before, they'd been one big blur and I hadn't even known it.

It was a wondrous thing, seeing each leaf outlined as its own entity, understanding the shape and form of things around me, appreciating their uniqueness and beauty. Everything that had been one mishmash suddenly appeared distinctly formed, and I felt in awe of it, as if I'd been transported into a world that had been there all along and escaped my notice. How could I have not seen clearly? How could definition make color brighter?

I'd been worried about how I would look in the glasses, how others would see me (and let's face it, the new look wasn't pretty with those black pointy frames with silver stars in the corners). I hadn't anticipated that I would see everything around me so differently. Temporarily, at least, I forgot to be self-conscious about my looks.

That's what seems to be happening now. A few days ago, driving by dried-up fields and trees drooping with fatigue, I would have been overwhelmed with melancholy. Today I saw the same thing as lovely. Obviously the view hasn't changed. But something in me has. I'm seeing things in a new way, and I'm not sure why. If it's due to the pearls, it's a side effect Dr. Edelman never mentioned.

It was most profound on the landing in Seattle. I've visited many times over the years, but this morning, flying in around eleven a.m., the sun dazzled me. We circled over Puget Sound, decreasing in altitude with each loop as though we were descending into a vortex of light. The sun sparkled on the water, almost blinding me. I've visited at times in rainy, gray weather. But today I felt like the plane gently lowered me into a cavern of diamonds. That's how brilliant and beautiful it was.

Holly and Becky met me at the airport. Becky reminds me a lot of Rose, or what I think she would have looked like at fifteen. Holly and Phil named her for the flower Rudbeckia, the brown-eyed Susan. Sure enough, she has brown eyes and beautiful blond hair. Her name is not officially Rudbeckia, though—they wouldn't have done that to her. And Holly didn't have as much investment in carrying on the family flower lineage as I did.

She's tall and thin, still at that stage halfway between tomboy and princess. She's the girl I always envied in school. The one with hair that falls in gentle waves over her shoulders. One minute she's got it pulled back into a ponytail with a scrunchie. And the next it's wrapped up in a tousle on top of her head. It's like seeing an ever-changing hologram of her many sides.

Holly looks no different than ever. Seattle has always

suited her well. She's tan, even though she lives in a place notorious for clouds, and she walks the hills around her house four miles a day, so she's always fit.

I hadn't realized how much I missed her until I saw her and Becky waving when I got to the terminal.

"I can't believe you're here!" she said. "This may be the most spontaneous thing you've ever done. We only talked a few days ago, and now you're here in the flesh."

That was when I started to cry. It caught me totally unaware, but I hugged her and didn't want to let go.

"I'm so glad to see you," I said. "I didn't realize how much I missed you."

I noticed that she and Becky were sparkling, just like the cavern of diamonds, just like the leaves on the trees. More and more, just like everything around me.

The drive to Holly's house felt like an awakening. With all the greenery and flowers in full bloom, the world seemed to be living and breathing again. Such an extraordinary change from the dying at home.

Every breath was filled with life from the sea and the fertile ground, the scent of flowers and shrubs. I didn't realize how parched I was.

Walking into Holly's house always feels like coming home, even though it's the exact opposite of Mama's house. I suppose because it's a reflection of Holly, because there's so much of her and Phil and the kids in it.

Huge windows overlook Puget Sound, and everything is painted white. She has filled it with so much color and texture, though, that there's nothing stark about it. The pine floors mellow more every time I see them, and the melon colors of the furniture and pillows and rugs and paintings give the place a perennial optimism. It's the perfect antidote to Seattle's gloomiest days, feeling as if you're inside a carton of sherbet.

My favorites are the touches she brought back with her from Mama's after the funeral. She wanted the glass chicken canisters—the ones with rooster heads on the lids. We packed those together, nesting them in Styrofoam peanuts and bubble wrap to make sure they arrived safely. They survived Holly and me growing up, and now her kids.

She's also got four of Mama's quilts, which are always on the beds. She wanted me to keep the Flower Garden quilt, the one that Mama started when she was a teenager and finished when she finally had time forty years later. But she has the Wedding Ring, the Flying Geese, and two Log Cabin quilts. And then there's the cut-glass vase. She keeps it on the kitchen island filled with flowers. Today it held a bouquet of coneflowers that she bought in the Market.

Phil and the boys were out when we got to the house, and Becky had made plans with friends, so Holly and I had time to ourselves for a few hours.

"I thought we'd have sandwiches here for lunch and then go exploring," Holly said. "There's a new little boutique I want to take you to. And maybe we'll go to the spa to get our nails done."

"Sure," I said, digging in a drawer for silverware while she got out the bread and tuna salad. "I'm up for anything."

"You look great," she said, glancing at me while she took plates down from the cupboard. "I mean, you always look good, but you have a glow about you now. And when did you get that mole removed?"

So here it was already. Decision time. Would I tell her or not? I helped her pour glasses of tea, trying to hide my awkwardness.

"I just thought it was time for it to go away," I said. Not exactly a lie. Not exactly the truth.

"Well, life must be agreeing with you," Holly said as we

sat at the island to eat. "Or is it a man in your life?" Nothing like a sister to go straight for the heart.

"Oh, lord, no," I said.

"Well," Holly said, "Phil has a new associate. A great guy. Been divorced a couple of years. I thought we might invite him for dinner while you're here."

I had no uncertainty about my answer to this one. "No, really, please, I just want to spend time with you and Phil and the kids. I want to use the time I have with you, not a stranger."

"Okay, sure," Holly said, handing me a bowl of sliced avocado. "Ever hear from Joe?"

"As a matter of fact, I got a card from him the other day. You know Joe—he always sends me a card around the time Mama died. I'm going to see him when I get back."

"Really?" she said, with a bit of extra energy. "I got an e-mail from him not long ago. He asked about you."

I took a sip of tea. "You still keep in touch?"

"Sure," Holly said. "You know we've always loved Joe. I never completely understood what happened between you two. Do you think you'll ever want to talk about it?"

"Maybe I'll surprise you sometime," I said. "But not today. Let's change the subject."

The night Rose died, Joe and I drove home from the hospital in silence. I looked out the car window at the moon rising, present even though the sun hadn't yet disappeared over the horizon.

It was the moment between day and night, the junction of light and darkness. I had always felt a safe equilibrium of those two emotions in me, but now my entire life tipped dangerously out of balance.

I kept expecting to hear Rose's voice from the backseat. I expected to hear her hum or sing or talk about the butterflies she hoped to see at camp that summer.

Instead, I heard Joe's voice. Quiet, as though he didn't want to fracture the silence.

"Do we need to stop at the store for anything?" he said.

I stared at him as though he'd lost his mind. It was just his way, of course. He wanted to make sure we had something to eat in the morning. Rose would want us to take care of ourselves.

But to raise such an insignificant question in the face of our enormous loss struck me as heartless. His preparation had not kept our daughter alive. All of his efforts to keep us safe had not worked.

"Our daughter just died, Joe," I wanted to say. "And you're concerned about whether we'll have eggs for breakfast?" I wanted to spit the words at him, to destroy him with my pain.

"No," I said quietly, staring ahead at the highway.

That was the moment. That was the moment when I started to bend his strength against him, to reshape his words and meaning to hurt me since I could never, ever hurt myself enough.

I remember when Holly and I were in elementary school, and we desperately wanted to take dance lessons. Mama didn't have the money, and we knew better than to press her on it, so we decided to teach ourselves.

We mimicked everything we saw in the movies and on TV, from the go-go dancers in white kidskin boots to the penguin waddle in *Mary Poppins*. We twirled and jumped and pranced to our own choreography, not to some tightly structured routine. We'd put on some of Mama and Daddy's old albums of *West Side Story* and *My Fair Lady* and fling ourselves around the living room in what we thought were the most graceful moves this side of Julie Andrews.

We turned the flowered couch in the living room into our stage, but we only used it when Mama wasn't around.

We moved the coffee table out of the way and jumped off the front and back of the couch, floating for a moment before our feet hit the ground and we went running across the room, our chests puffed out, our heads held high, and our arms trailing behind us like Audrey Hepburn.

Mama was in her early thirties then, too young to be a widow but too old to be carefree. Stuck somewhere in between with two girls to feed. Sometimes late at night, when Holly and I were supposed to be asleep, I'd lie awake and hear her cleaning up the kitchen or punching the buttons on her adding machine. She'd do her paperwork for the antiques business at the kitchen table, listening to her favorite song on the stereo. It was "I'll Never Find Another You," the original version by the Seekers, with its perfect harmony and imploring vocals. She listened to it over and over.

Finally the music would stop, the light under the door would go out, and I'd hear her humming the song to herself as she went to bed alone.

I hope I didn't offend Holly, but I really wasn't "up for anything" after all. I talked her out of the boutique and spa and asked her if we could go to a botanical garden instead. I needed the green and the peace. And the time to talk without sorting through clothing racks or having cotton balls stuffed between our toes.

She kept looking at me out of the corner of her eye, as though she saw something different in me. I haven't noticed big changes in the mirror, but apparently more has changed than I realize.

We wandered the garden shrouded in mist, but every once in a while the sun broke through and turned the serene into the spectacular. We had the gardens almost to ourselves, and every plant spoke to me. I could almost hear their voices. Their energy and vitality and joy. Incredible joy. The voice of something that has everything it needs. The sound of thriving.

We stopped at a bed of roses with blooms as big as dinner plates.

"What do you think Rose would be doing now?" Holly asked. She had a way of drawing me out about Rose so I wouldn't keep it all stopped-up inside. She'd told me long ago that she would always continue to talk about her so she would be present for both of us.

The collective scent of the roses overwhelmed me, and I leaned over to smell a white hybrid tea rose labeled PRISTINE.

"I think she would be here with us," I said. "Maybe she'd be married, have a baby or two. I like to think she'd be very, very happy."

"Yeah, that's all we really want for our kids, isn't it?" Holly said. "That's what it all comes down to."

And that was when I decided not to say anything to her about the unhappiness that led to the pearls.

The pearls. As I breathed in the rich scent all around me, I wondered for the first time why they were green, the color of life.

DAY ELEVEN

Being at Holly's is the biggest gift, and it's the most excruciating thing I could do. Her life is intact. Phil loves her and is a good father to the kids. Mark will be off to college in a few days. Brent's been mowing lawns all summer. And Becky is spending lots of time with her friends, buying back-to-school clothes. Holly has her volunteer work and keeps everything running.

It all seems so easy. It's what I thought my life would be. How did mine take such different turns? I'm happy for her, I really am. But why does her life keep increasing, while mine keeps ebbing away?

As we fixed supper, Phil told me about the work he's doing. "I may come to a symposium in Ames next spring," he said. "Mind if I come stay with you for a couple of days while I'm there?"

Another not knowing. I guess we never know whether we'll be here six months from now, or even six minutes from now, but having a strong likelihood of it is so different from my situation.

"Sure," I said, thinking how much I'd enjoy that.

It seems that I'm more alive now than ever, attracting

good things even though I'm not trying. It's as though someone turned on a neon light over my head that says, "Talk to her. Come see her." I even found a hundred-dollar bill on the plane yesterday. I gave it to Holly and told her to get something for the kids with it.

"And Mark is graduating next spring, so we'd love to have you come out here for that," Holly said.

"Nothing would make me happier," I told her. At least I could be honest about that.

"Phil has been e-mailing Joe," Holly told me. We were chopping vegetables for stir-fry. "I hope that's okay," she said. "Joe's a great resource, so Phil has gotten his opinion on a couple of projects."

"Sure," I said, "of course that's okay."

Holly offered me a glass of wine while we cooked.

"It was so sweet of him to send you that card," Holly said. "So when are the two of you getting together?"

"On Tuesday," I said, picturing the calendar with the red Xs and big red circle on the wall at home.

"Did he tell you about Carol?" Phil asked.

Holly gave him a look.

"No," I said. "But from the return address, I noticed they must have moved."

"Well, I don't know if he'd want us to say something to you," Holly said, looking again at Phil. "But Joe moved. Carol didn't," she said. "They're getting a divorce."

I put my knife down and hung on to the edge of the counter. "Really?" I said, taking a deep breath. "What happened?"

"I don't know," Holly said. "He mentioned it to Phil, so I got the news secondhand."

"That's a shame," I said, almost meaning it. "They always seemed good together."

"But nothing like the two of you," Holly said.

I went back to my chopping.

"I'm sorry . . . that just slipped out."

"No reason not to tell the truth," I said, realizing the irony of that.

"So can I ask you . . . why *did* the two of you split up?" Holly said. "To be honest, I never really understood it. I figured you had good reasons, and I know it's hard for couples who have lost a child. But when you two had so much history together, I thought that might see you through."

"Sometimes history isn't enough," I said, scooping the vegetables into the pan on the stove. "Want me to set the table?"

We spent the morning at the locks in the ship canal. We go every time I visit, but I never get tired of watching the transition of boats from salt water to fresh. It's all so big, so orchestrated. Like poetry.

The weather was breezy and warm. Sea spray pelted our hair and dampened our clothes. I could feel my lungs taking in the fresh air, filling with something besides the dust from the gravel roads back home.

I'm starting to see the number 20 everywhere. I had never thought about the fact that Holly's street address is 2020. Perfect vision. We went to a Chinese restaurant for lunch, and the dish I wanted was number 20.

When we got back, Holly's dog, Shannon, followed me everywhere through the house. She's a spaniel-collie mix, so she's bred to herd, but Holly said she'd never seen anything like it. "She's drawn to you," she said. "Like there's something magnetic. Or she's watching over you."

I noticed this all day long. I'm staying in their guest room, and in the afternoon I stretched out to read while Holly made phone calls for a charity event she's running. Shannon lay on the bed next to me, and one by one, the kids came into the room and sat down to talk.

I've never had Mama's gift of gab. But maybe I was a

priest in a former life, and people still feel called to confess, even when I can't.

Becky came first.

"Am I bothering you, Aunt Meg?" she said, poking her head in the door. She saw I was reading, not sleeping.

"Not at all, sweetie," I said, glad to have some time with her alone. "Come on in." Becky was only six months old when Holly and Phil and the kids moved to Seattle. I've never had the time with her that I did with the boys, yet I feel closer to her. Maybe because the beginning of her life was so linked with the end of my daughter's.

She sat down in the chair by the window with the view of the water and pulled her legs up under her. Her hair cascaded over her shoulders, reminding me of Mama's hair— and what Rose's would have been like, too.

"So what's new in your life, Rudbeckia?" I said, sitting up straighter. I laid my reading glasses on the bedside table and patted Shannon on the head to reassure her I wasn't leaving.

Becky smiled and twisted a strand of hair in her fingers. I was the only one she allowed to call her by her would-be floral name.

"Well," she said, "school starts in a couple of weeks, so that's exciting. And kind of scary."

"You'll be a sophomore, right?" I said. "So what's the exciting part, and what's the scary part? Besides, oh . . . everything?"

She smiled again and looked up at the ceiling, trying to find a place to start. "I'll be on the varsity soccer team, so that's exciting. The scary part is . . . well, there are a lot of scary parts."

"Any of them have to do with a boy?" I asked, surprising myself. Maybe my shortened timeline is making me more direct.

"Yeeeees," she said, gathering her hair on top of her head and letting it fall down again. "His name's Devon."

"How long have you known him?" I asked.

"Just since spring. He transferred in last year from California." She shifted in her seat and hung her legs over the side of the chair.

"And have you been dating?"

"Not really . . . not yet. Just group dates. Going to games and out for pizza and stuff."

"Do your parents know about him?"

"No. I mean, they know who he is. He's been here to the house with a bunch of other kids. But they don't know there's anything special between us."

"And how do *you* know there's something special?"

She blushed and looked out the window, then pulled her knees up to her chest. "I just really like him. He's smart and easy to talk to. He talks about real stuff, you know? Not like he's trying to impress me."

"All good qualities," I said. "And . . . he's cute?"

She blushed again.

"Well . . . of course," she said, beaming.

"So the scary part is that maybe he doesn't like you as much as you like him," I said. "And the other scary part is that he does."

Becky looked me right in the eye. "How did you know that?" she said.

"Experience," I said. "Everything that's exciting has an edge of fear to it. The trick is to follow the excitement, not the fear. I mean, make good decisions, but don't let your fear stop you."

Shannon opened her eyes, her head still on her paws, and looked at me, as if to say, "You do realize, don't you, that you're talking to yourself?"

Maybe some of Joe's guidance rubbed off on me all those years ago.

Becky's phone rang. She glanced at it and smiled. "It's him," she said. "Thanks, Aunt Meg." She kissed my cheek as she left.

A few minutes later, Mark knocked on the guest room door and came in and sat down. We talked about his senior year in college, his internship, the young woman from Taiwan he's been dating, what his plans are after graduation.

And then, shortly after he left, same thing with Brent. He told me he's been struggling in school and wondering if he should take a year off. He may not have come to any conclusions, but it seemed helpful for him to talk it through.

Such good kids, and I'm so grateful to have had that time with them. Holly and Phil have done a tremendous job raising them. Their grandmother—and their cousin— would be proud.

Holly and I set out the stir-fry and rice, and we sat around the kitchen table telling stories. All three of the kids were here for supper before they went out for the evening, and it seemed like the right time to give them the mementos I'd brought.

A music box for Becky that belonged to Mama. A level for Brent from Daddy's toolbox that Mama used all the time. And a blue ribbon from Daddy's spelling bee days for Mark.

"These are so cool," they said as they opened them, genuinely touched. It's one of the things I love most about them—their capacity for gratitude and valuing things that other kids wouldn't.

"Well, the items are great in and of themselves," I said. "But they mean a lot more when you know the stories behind them."

"Do you remember that level, Holly?" I said, picking it up and tilting it back and forth until the fluid centered in the middle of the little glass window.

"Oh, heavens, yes," she said. "Sometimes I thought Mama would beat us over the head with it just to get us to help her out in the barn."

"What was she doing?" Brent asked.

Funny how one question can be like a faucet just waiting to turn on a whole conversation. For the next hour, Holly and I recalled the first few years after Daddy died, and how Mama held on to that acreage, determined to live out as much of their dream as she could.

We told them how Mama and Daddy bought the place with plans for more children, big gardens; it was a place with room for hobbies and horses. The dream of a bigger family died with Daddy, of course, but Mama held on to that acreage with the little bit of insurance money she collected.

How she managed it, we don't really know. But she set to work selling vegetables that she raised. And she'd go to garage sales and buy broken-down old furniture and take it to the barn to repair it, talking to Romeo for company. Then she'd sell it out of the barn, freshly upholstered and painted. She called it Fleur Antiques to make it sound respectable. She knew how to make things new again.

"Do you remember Grandpa at all?" Becky asked Holly and me. I smiled at her curiosity. Daddy and Rose were both phantoms in her mind since they were gone before she was born. Only Mama held real memories for her.

We'd moved into the living room, where Becky stretched out on the couch and put her feet in Holly's lap. Sometimes I thought she might be sleeping. But I think she took it all in, weaving pieces of memories into some kind of braid she could hold on to, connecting her to all that came before.

"Barely," Holly said. "I was only three when he died. Mostly I remember him being happy. And didn't we go to drive-in movies?" she asked me.

"We did. I'm surprised you remember that. You always fell asleep right after the show started."

"I remember how he'd come home at the end of the day wearing a suit and fedora—looking very dapper," I said. "He'd give Mama a kiss and pick up Holly and me and swing us around in the kitchen. And then he'd go change clothes as fast as he could, as if he couldn't wait to get into his work clothes and go out to tinker in the barn.

"The acreage always had something that needed to be fixed, and he loved to do it. He'd come in with grease on his T-shirt, and Mama would scold him, even though she never really seemed mad. Then she'd peel that shirt off him right there in the kitchen and treat it with ammonia and white vinegar."

"How do you remember that?" Holly said.

"Oh, Mama taught me all those tricks," I said.

"How come you didn't learn those things, Mom?" Brent said, teasing.

"Your grandma tried to teach her," I said, "but your mom was too busy with the boys."

Phil smiled, and Becky opened her eyes and came to life. "Those are the stories we really want to hear," she said, waving her feet in the air.

"Oh no, you don't," Holly said. "I was a model teenager." Her kids groaned in unison. "Anyway, as I recall, your aunt won the popularity award."

"Yeah, but everyone I dated broke up with me so they could date you," I said.

"Never mind," Holly said, trying to redirect the conversation. "Remember the home movies Daddy took of us?"

Sure, I remembered. The long bar of lights that attached to the movie camera, lighting up the living room at Christmas to film Holly and me when we opened our presents. The lights were so bright we squinted when he told us to look at the camera.

"I put those on DVDs a few years ago. Didn't I send a set to you?"

"You did," Holly said, getting up from the couch. "We haven't watched them in ages." She opened a cupboard under the bookshelves and pulled out the DVDs.

"Since we're talking about Daddy, I want to find the one where he's singing."

I smiled. "You mean the mash-up of 'Davy Crockett' and 'Wouldn't It Be Loverly'?"

"That's the one," she said. She handed a DVD to Mark, who loaded it into the player. Then she forwarded it to the scene she wanted.

There he was. Our dad, standing in the living room next to the old flowered couch. He wore a bearskin cap like Davy Crockett, and he sang in a booming baritone: "Born on a mountaintop in Tennessee, greenest state in the land of the free. . . ."

Then he paused while he took off the cap and picked up a broom like My Fair Lady and continued in a high-pitched voice . . . "warm face, warm hands, warm feet, oh, wouldn't it be loverly?"

Holly and I were off camera, but you could hear us squealing. "Sing it again, Daddy!"

"He loved making us laugh, didn't he?" Holly said.

"Definitely," I said. "That's what I remember most about him. He wanted us to be happy."

As we talked tonight, I could see beyond the kids' appearance to something deeper. I'd forgotten how it felt to sit and visit with the family. To be in the company of people I love. This house is so filled with life, and the farmhouse back home is so filled with memories. No wonder I thought my life was over.

The kids all had places to go. And Phil disappeared to the bedroom to read. "I'll let you two catch up," he said, giving Holly a kiss on the cheek.

Holly and I curled up on the couches, watching the

moonlight glance off the water. "It's beautiful here," I said. "You've created a wonderful life for yourself."

"Thanks," Holly said. "I try to never take it for granted." She turned and looked at me. "I want you to find happiness again, too. You deserve it more than anyone I know."

"I'm getting there," I said. "Day by day."

We were quiet for a minute. "I'll be right back," I said.

I went to my room and came back with the childhood picture I'd had enlarged. "I found something I want you to have," I said, handing her the tissue-wrapped box.

She unwrapped it, then held it and stared.

"I haven't seen this picture for ages," she said. "Where was it?"

"In a box in the basement," I said. "With a lot of other photos, and some of Daddy's things."

"We were so little," she said. "We had no idea, really."

I sat down quietly.

"How did Mama do it?" she asked. "How did she keep everything going? How did she make life good for us when she was devastated?"

At that moment, I felt a pain in my stomach. I hadn't thought about it this way. Mama hadn't given up. Ever. Even during the most difficult times. But she'd had us to keep her going. That made a difference, didn't it?

"I don't know," I said. "She was an exceptional woman. Anyway, I wanted you to have this. A reminder of the two of us, together always."

DAY TWELVE

I almost told Holly about the pearls today. It took all the restraint I had to keep from blurting it out. But she'd be horrified. And then she'd call every doctor in Seattle. So instead we went to see a healer. I felt exactly like Becky—excited and scared.

The sign on the shop said LIN CHOW: PRIVATE READINGS. We saw it after lunch, when we were trudging up Stewart Street with our hands full from the Market. The smell of sea air and fresh fish made me feel invigorated and alive. If we'd been smart, we would have done our shopping after lunch so we wouldn't have so much to carry. That was when the sign caught my eye. The number on the door said 2000, and I told Holly I wanted to go in.

She's never had a sense of the mystical like Mama and I did. She's not judgmental about it, but she is rooted firmly in this world. When we were little, she used to listen to my stories of fairies and trolls and elves and think that I made them up, when I was just telling her what I knew to be true outside our back door. I think she's always wanted to believe, really, but it's simply not in her makeup. She's sensitive, but completely sensible. Give her the choice between poetry or a good cookbook, and she'll choose the how-to every time.

So when I told her I wanted to go in and see Lin Chow, she just smiled and said, "Sure."

When we walked in, I started to tingle. I could feel that inner knowing, like a divining rod that starts to sway as you get closer to water. Lin nodded at Holly, then turned to me and bowed, as though she'd been expecting me.

On the ledge in front of the window, ceramic pots held an assortment of orchids, exotic cactus plants, and unexpected combinations of spiky agave and wandering Jew. The red curtains cast a rosy light throughout the room, and everything seemed to shimmer with vitality. It felt like a womb of peace and tranquility.

I knew the space made Holly uncomfortable, but I breathed it in like warm rain. I could tell I was with someone who understood what it means to have one foot in this world and one foot on the other side.

Lin's hair was swept up in a bun, and she wore a flowered tunic and black pants with sandals. She stood a head shorter than me, yet she had a large and peaceful presence.

Her first words were not, "How can I help you?" or "What can I do for you?" but "I'm glad you've come. Please sit." She motioned toward a tufted chair that faced a small ebony desk with carved legs.

"Please—" She motioned for Holly to sit on a flowered sofa under the window. "Sisters?" she said, looking back and forth at us.

"Yes," I said, knowing we don't look that much alike.

"Thank you," Holly said, "but I think I'll leave you alone for a few minutes. I've got an errand to run up the street. Is that okay?"

"Sure," I said.

"Yes," Lin said. "Thirty minutes, please."

Holly winked at me and headed back out into the sunlight.

I was happy Holly had left. I didn't want to reveal too much in front of her, but I also didn't want to be evasive. Mostly I just wanted to be with Lin and absorb that comforting energy. So clean and pure, it felt as though it was channeled directly from the other side.

She understood without my saying anything. "I will tell you only what you are open to hearing," she said. "Please, shuffle these cards."

I wasn't even sure what she planned to do. These weren't tarot cards—just an ordinary deck of playing cards. She wasn't a palm reader, or an energy healer. I shuffled the cards and handed them to her. She closed her eyes, took a couple of deep breaths, and laid out several cards in front of her. Then she picked them up and put them back in the deck. I realized they were nothing but a prop, like a string of rosary beads or a worry doll. They gave her body something to focus on so her mind could travel.

She opened her eyes and looked toward me, but through me, focusing on something in the distance. Her hands dealt out the cards and picked them up silently, but with a rhythm.

"You were born in October, no?" she asked.

"Yes," I said. "The ninth."

"Yes," she said. "Under a full moon. You have always been divinely protected."

"Really?" I said, surprised. "I haven't always felt that way."

"You have always been accompanied by beings of light," she said. "Does this make sense?"

I remembered Mama telling me that the colored swirls would always be with me. Was it possible, even if I couldn't see them? Even if the colors on my kitchen wall were my only reminder?

"Yes," I said. "It does."

"You are only in your body part of the time," Lin Chow continued. "You are one who travels frequently in other worlds. And you have experienced many losses, have you not?"

I said, "Yes," softly.

"One who is especially dear to you is here and wants to say hello," she said.

"My daughter?" I asked, eager for the answer to be yes.

"No," she said, "it is a masculine figure. A father figure."

"Daddy?" I wondered.

"Yes," she said, "he was your father in this life, but you have been apart for many years, have you not?"

"Yes, that's right."

"He is concerned about you," she said.

I stiffened.

"He knows you have made a decision that may not be the best for you. Does this make sense?"

"Yes," I said.

"He is close by you and wants you to know that." She kept dealing and picking up the cards.

"The decision," I said, ". . . does he have information about how the decision will turn out?"

She paused for a moment, listening intently. "He cannot say," she said. "He is shaking his head."

I took a deep breath.

"But he has something for you," she said. "It is a rose. It appears to be very meaningful. Does this make sense?"

"Yes," I said. "It does."

She dealt the cards more slowly and intently now.

"There is something you want to ask, is there not?" she said.

I looked up at the ceiling. "You know when I was born," I said slowly, not sure I wanted the answer to the next question. "Do you also know when I will leave this life?"

She laid out seven cards on the table, then picked them up again. "This information is never shared," she said quietly. "It is a law of the universe. Only God knows the answer to this question."

Was she being honest, or did she have information she didn't want to share?

"It is the truth," she said, as though she heard my silent question.

"I can tell you this," she said. "There is something in you that doesn't belong. You must get rid of it or you will die."

Same rhythm of cards on the table. Same peaceful quiet in the room.

I took another deep breath. "Can you tell me what it is?" I said.

She reached across the table and took my hands in hers.

"Your chi energy is strong and alive," she said. "And at the same time it tells me an ending is coming soon."

"Have you felt this before?" I asked.

"Not in quite this way," she said. "But I can tell you that one's system is most vital just before an important change."

I felt exposed, as though she knew my secret. When I looked away, she picked up the cards, straightened the deck, and set it on the table with a sense of finality. "You have this answer," she said. "You are the only one who knows."

I sat quietly.

"But I have something that may help you," she said. She got up, walked to a carved wooden cabinet on the other side of the room, and pulled out a packet filled with powder.

"Drink this with your food," she said. "Stir it into liquid. It will help you."

Did she know somehow about the pearls? Was this an

antidote of some kind? I thought of the lab tests and what they might show. *Yes, doctor,* I imagined myself saying. *My red blood count was low, so I drank a white powder from a Chinese healer. Of course, that was after I took a bottle of pearls that might kill me.*

I heard the jingle of bells as Holly came back in the shop.

"You are right on time," Lin said, rising from her chair, indicating that we were done. I felt like I'd been there for hours, and I could barely move to stand up. But I turned around and smiled at Holly.

"Did you get what you needed?" I asked. I pulled cash out of my purse and handed it to Lin.

"Sure thing," she said. "I hope you did, too."

Lin smiled and bowed toward each of us. "Good day," she said. "Take good care of one another. This is what sisters do."

I've been part of a sisterhood in many ways, and its gifts are not lost on me. The spring after Mama died, I planted a memorial garden for her and Rose under the pergola behind the house.

Nancy and I stayed at the shop a couple of nights after closing, and she helped me design the bed. I brought in the measurements, and we drew it out on graph paper, the way Mama used to do. We chose shade-loving perennials with foliage ranging from deep emerald to variegations of celery green and white. Lily of the valley for its sweet scent in early spring, bleeding heart for its delicate pink blooms in May and June, and lamium to fill in between the plants and cover the ground with green.

We filled up my backseat three times with all the nursery stock and put bags of compost in the trunk.

"Want some help planting?" she said. "I could come over Sunday and spend the day. We could get it all done."

"Thanks," I said, "but I think I want to do this part

alone." Mama always taught me that if you plant flowers with love, they'll grow better, and I know that's true.

I wanted to make a ritual out of digging the hole for each plant. I'd mixed up some liquid fertilizer, and before I lowered each plant in the ground, I talked to it, baptized its roots with the fertilizer, then gently packed loose dirt around it to give it stability and contact with the soil.

I was just about done when Nancy drove up in the van from the shop.

I stood up, peeled off my garden gloves, and went to give her a hug.

"I hope I'm not interrupting," she said. "I just wanted to stop by and give you something."

"Your timing is great," I said. "I've had a good day out here, but I'm ready for a break."

Nancy looked over the bed and smiled. "It's really coming together, isn't it?" she said.

I stood back and looked at it for the first time. I'd been so busy studying each individual plant that I hadn't seen the harmony from a distance. "I guess so," I said.

"Well, hopefully you can find a spot for this," Nancy said, opening the back of the van. There, propped up by boxes and cushioned by blankets, was a birdbath in the shape of an angel. The face, with its half-open eyes and delicate lips, conveyed tranquility and rest, and the wings folded together in front to form the basin.

"Oh my God, Nancy. That's beautiful," I said. "You brought that for me?"

"Of course," she said. "I ordered it into the shop and then hid it from you the last few days. As soon as I saw it, I knew it belonged to you—and to Rose and your mom."

We stood and stared at it, in all its concrete weightiness, both thinking the same thing.

"I bet you had some help getting it in there, didn't you?" I said.

Nancy nodded.

"And I bet we're going to need some help getting it out of there."

"Right," she said, clearly embarrassed that she hadn't thought things through.

"Okay," I said. "I'll call Miriam."

Ten minutes later, Miriam showed up wearing sturdy shoes and carrying a bottle of wine, and the three of us heaved the angel out of the van and into a spot where the freshly planted hosta and astilbe would eventually surround it in a sea of green.

"Nice work, ladies," Miriam said.

We pulled up lawn chairs near the pergola and spent the rest of the afternoon together. I considered it the best consecration the garden could have.

DAY THIRTEEN

On the way to the airport this morning, I stared out the car window, trying to drink up as much of the vitality of the vine-covered overpasses and landscaped lawns as I could. "I forgot how much I like it here," I said.

"You could move out here, you know," Holly said. "There's nothing really stopping you."

I paused. "You know, it would be so hard to leave home. So many memories there."

"Maybe it would be good to get away from those."

"Maybe," I said.

Holly and I have had this conversation before. "Why don't you move out here near us? In fact, you can move in with us if you want. The kids would love it, and so would I."

"You know how attached I am to home," I said. "You'd have to move heaven and earth to get me away from there."

I remembered what waited for me back on the acreage. Not the usual rolling hills, the green, the enchantment, as though nature was talking to me. But plants barely hanging on, even the leaves on the trees suffering and withering.

The day I left for Seattle, leaves from the river birch covered the deck—at least a month ahead of schedule. And the cottonwood trees—the ones in the small grove that Rose and I used to call the fairy circle—showed signs of stress with brown leaves curling before they fell to the ground.

"That's a big house for you to take care of all by yourself," Holly said.

"Most of the time, I like keeping it up," I said honestly. "I don't like the repair work, but you know how I am. Anything in the yard, whether it's a hundred degrees or ten below zero, that's my joy."

Well, not completely truthful. I hadn't been used to twelve days of 100-plus temperatures in a row.

"You'll have to tell me how things go with Joe," Holly said. "Are you excited to see him?"

"Yes," I said, realizing the truth in my response. "And nervous, too." Also true.

Before I left the house, I left a note for each of the kids under their pillow, expressing how much I admire them and love them. I didn't want the notes to sound like I was saying good-bye, just encouragement from their favorite aunt.

When we got to the airport, my flight flew out of gate B20.

As the plane landed, the pilot announced the time: three o'clock. And the temperature: 102 degrees. I retrieved the car and drove home under a bright blue sky with no clouds in sight, reentering a world still petrified by heat and drought.

How often have I wished for this on a cold January day? But this year the heat feels relentless and cruel, especially after Seattle, where my senses started to fill up with color and fragrance again. Here it smells like everything is dying. Even the rows of corn, which typically would be robust, standing tall and glossy green this time of year, are withered and gray.

I feel like I went to another world, and one I needed to visit to remind myself that this acreage, as much as I love it, is not all there is. I made my decision based on the withering around me and in me. And now I've gone to another place that's vibrant and alive, where I could feel glimmers of the same qualities in myself again. So do I regret my decision to take the pearls? I'm still not fully sure. I know saying good-bye to Holly was one of the most difficult things I've ever done.

When I got home, I pulled the car onto the shoulder of the highway to get the mail. A hot wind whipped my hair as I leaned out of the car and reached into the box to tease out the accumulation of circulars and bills. Then I sat back and flipped through the stack, looking for one thing: the lab results.

They weren't there. I went through the stack again piece by piece, thinking I must have missed it, but nothing.

I leaned back in the seat and closed my eyes, feeling the weight of every minute that has passed, and every minute I may have remaining. The wind kicked up dust and burned my eyes, and I felt my legs weaken beneath me.

Don't panic, I told myself. *Patience. Remember all the joy of the past few days. Remember. Remember. Remember.*

When I got to the house, I found a note tucked inside the screen door. It was from Joe.

It felt good to know he'd been here, had seen Mama's driveway and porch. Maybe he'd sat on the porch swing to write the note. I went inside, turned up the air-conditioning to cool off the place and clear out the stuffiness, and sat down at the kitchen table to read the note. It looked as if he wrote it on whatever scrap of paper he had in the car.

I'm looking forward to seeing you, it said. *I'll give you a call to make plans.*

One summer when Rose was seven years old, we went camping at a state park. Joe and Rose went off into the woods on one of their scavenger hunts while I made supper on the camp stove. I heard a crash and a scream, and I went running until I found Rose on the ground, Joe bent over her.

"She fell off that log," he said, motioning to a dead tree. Rose bit her lip but didn't cry.

"Where does it hurt?" Joe asked her.

"My ankle," she said, trying to sit up.

"Stay still," I said, crouching next to her and stroking her face. Dirt and leaves clung to her hair.

Joe gingerly felt her ankle. "It's not broken," he said. "I think you're going to live." She smiled and slowly sat up.

"Want a ride?" Joe said. He squatted down in front of her, and I helped lift her onto his back.

He walked carefully back to the campsite, picking his way through the woods, while Rose reached up and brushed away low-hanging foliage. We wrapped her ankle with an elastic bandage from the first aid kit, and by the next day, she was skipping around as if nothing had happened.

I knew the accident wasn't Joe's fault—and Rose didn't suffer any real injuries. But a voice inside me urged me to blame someone, and he was the only person available.

It strikes me as no accident that he would show up now. It's time to make amends as I should have done long ago.

Rose wanted to be an astronaut. She made the announcement when we were all out in the backyard on a typical Saturday morning. I weeded the garden, Joe trimmed the boxwood hedge, Rose swung on the swing set, going higher and higher, and Cricket stretched out, relaxed but alert under the linden tree, watching Rose's every move, as usual.

She announced her life ambition out of the blue, at the top of her lungs, declaring her purpose to the clouds and the trees and to God Himself.

"I'M GOING TO BE AN AS-TRO-NAUT!" she said, then jumped off the swing and landed on her feet. She climbed right back on and started kicking her legs, sending the swing ever higher.

Joe and I looked at each other, tickled by what we had helped create.

"An astronaut?" Joe said. "What made you decide to be an astronaut?"

"Because," she said, pumping her legs and pushing the swing with her whole body, "there are bugs on other planets, and I want to find them." Then she jumped off the swing again and climbed right back on.

That night Joe got out Rose's pad of drawing paper and box of crayons and set them in front of her on the kitchen table.

"So what do you think those bugs from other planets look like?" he asked.

She grinned, energized by the challenge, grabbed a crayon, and started to draw. Thirty minutes later, we had seven detailed drawings of alien creatures. An orange spiderlike monster with fangs and claws. A pink-and-white-striped bug that looked like a fish, with gills that doubled as wings. An astounding purple worm that lived underground and laid two thousand eggs at once.

"These are beautiful," I said as I started hanging them on the refrigerator.

"Yes," Rose said as she sat back, scratched Cricket behind one ear, and admired her artwork. "But we have bugs that are just as beautiful right here on Earth."

* * *

When we came home from the hospital after Rose died, we drove up the gravel lane to our house inside a cloud of lightning bugs. We could see the twinkling lights before we even turned in the drive. Hundreds of them. Thousands, maybe. They surrounded our car as though they were delivering us to the door, to our new life without Rose.

When we got out of the car, we stood and watched for a few minutes as they continued to turn on and off, a field of ever-moving stars. Then, as though in unison, they disappeared, leaving us with the darkness and moonlight.

I walked up the steps to the door, where Cricket lay quiet, greeting us with a soft whimper that told me he knew his friend was gone. I felt as heavy as I had when I carried Rose in my womb. Joe followed me, flipping on the lights in the kitchen. The venom I'd felt in the car on the way home numbed me to his touch, to his glance.

Without looking at him or saying a word, I walked to Rose's room and turned on the light. Her latest artwork hung on the wall. Her braided friendship bracelets were stacked on her dresser. Next to the snowman jars of cotton balls sat another jar, the one she'd used to catch a lightning bug just three nights before.

I stopped breathing for a moment when I saw that jar. Rose captured bugs, but she fed them and let them go. She prided herself on taking care of them for just a short while, then returning them to the outdoors. "I'd like to keep them," she said, "but they have their own lives, you know?"

I walked to the dresser, picked up the jar with holes punched in the top, and looked inside. There the lightning bug lay on its back, already starting to decay.

I didn't know Joe was standing in the doorway, watching me. But when I started to weep, he came and held me. I wanted to melt into him the way I always had. But I didn't.

I stood straight and stiff, as though all that was left of me was a bag of bones.

After reading Joe's note when I got home, I sat and looked at the colors on the kitchen wall as if seeing them for the first time. They were more vibrant than I'd realized, yet peaceful. I felt myself blending with them somehow, embraced by their welcome.

When I got ready for bed, I sat on the toilet and noticed a fluffy white towel on the vanity in the glow of the night-light. A few days ago I would have thought, *Why didn't I put that in the laundry before I left for Seattle? Why can't I be a better housekeeper? Is laundry detergent on the list?* Instead, I looked at it and saw the way the texture and folds created curves and arcs, light and shadow.

I saw every contour and could feel the softness and comfort of the towel as though it were around my shoulders. I could see the essence of the towel in all its loveliness. It almost looked alive.

"Okay," I said to myself. "Now I'm really starting to lose it."

But I realized I was gaining something real and important instead.

I didn't drink the powder from the healer while I was at Holly's for fear of what effect it might have. So tonight, as I held the packet from Lin in my hand, it was time to make a decision.

After being so filled up by the trip, I felt the same sense of vacancy that had led me to take the pearls in the first place.

But at the same time, my vision has begun to change. Not my external vision, not the way I see the colored glass in the kitchen window or the slant of light from the moon, but something inside me. Either Seattle or the pearls has changed me. Even the thirsty grass and the drooping flowers, despite Miriam's care in my absence, affect me differently now. More and more, I'm filled with peace instead of sadness.

I've been depleted, as though a part of me has been dying for a long, long time. Another part of me is emerging into new life, and I've been resisting that and holding it in. It's time to let the new life arrive, even though it may cause some endings. This is the way of nature, and I'm willing to let nature take its course without more intervention, whatever the outcome.

Just a few days ago, I didn't know if my life was worth living. Then I didn't know if it was worth saving. Now I'm not sure it's worth throwing away. Having twenty days is so different from a sudden demise because I have time to question my decision, to prepare or resist. That's my choice.

I choose not to resist, but to prepare for whatever is to come. And the fascinating thing is that I understand now—the preparation to live is the same as the preparation to die. With all the cleaning out, I've learned not to hold on to things that I no longer need.

So tonight I sat down at the kitchen table, opened the packet of powder from Lin Chow, and stirred it into a glass of water. I stirred slowly and deliberately until all the crystals dissolved and disappeared, just like the pearls when I stirred them into the yogurt.

Then I carried the glass outside, poured it into a watering can, added more water, and sprinkled it on the flower beds, starting with the memorial garden. If there is new life in that powder, may it soak into the ground and nourish those flowers to the very depth of their roots.

DAY FOURTEEN

At 8:01 this morning, I called the clinic and told Carla the results haven't arrived yet.

"Really?" she said. "I'm sorry. They should have been there by now. Let me check on them for you."

I sat by the phone until she called back a few minutes later. "They were sent out last Wednesday," she said. "Maybe the mail is just slow. If they don't show up tomorrow, give me another call."

"Can I go ahead and find out what the tests showed?" I asked, feeling my heart beat faster.

"Sorry," she said. "The lab can't release the results except to the doctor, and he's out of the country on a family vacation."

I took a deep breath. "Okay, thank you," I said. "I'll let you know if they aren't here tomorrow."

Back and forth, back and forth. Last night I was so at peace about the powder. This morning I felt like I was in a cage, rattling the bars.

In my best moments, I feel better than I have in years. I don't know if this is a side effect of the pearls or of my own state of mind, but I feel a little giddy, as if I'm going on vacation and can't wait to get there. It feels totally irreverent to say that, but it's true, and I figure there's no reason for me not to be completely honest, at least with myself.

Why does life inspire us to be dishonest, as though pretending or lying will make anything better? When you have nothing to lose, you realize how much easier everything is when you just tell the truth.

So here it is—at least part of the time: I'm grateful for Dr. Edelman. And if anyone reads this after I'm gone and blames him, please try to understand my point of view and realize that he did nothing wrong. If you want to blame anyone, blame me. But, truly, there is no one to blame. I'm at peace with my decision. So energized, in fact, that I spent the evening washing out old flowerpots and gathering up miscellaneous tools, and I came to one profound conclusion:

This is one hell of a time to fall in love with my life.

The phone rang while I was unloading the clothes dryer, and I knew who it was before I picked it up. Joe.

"Hello?" I said, leaning against the washer.

"Hi, Meg," he said. "Am I catching you at a good time?"

"You are," I said. "You're saving me from folding clothes."

"Good," he said. "Glad I can help." His voice sounded warm as ever, but I heard noise in the background.

"Are you calling from your conference?" I asked.

"Yep, we're in between sessions, so I thought I'd see if I could catch you. How was your trip?"

"Great," I said. "Everybody's doing fine. Holly and Phil said to tell you hi."

"Maybe you can tell me all about it when we get together," he said. "How about Lulu's for lunch tomorrow?"

I paused, remembering all the times we went to Lulu's

for hamburgers when we first got married and couldn't afford anything fancier. That was fine with me. Some of our most romantic moments happened in the least fancy places: the hardware store, getting groceries, painting the front porch.

I remember one moment in the plumbing section at Miller's Hardware when we were teasing each other. I looked at him, and he seemed so strong and capable, and I trusted him so much, that I felt my soul expand beyond my body with happiness. Just pure contentment. That would happen every once in a while, and I always took it as a gift, even if I just felt it for a second. Some people, I figured, never feel it at all.

"Sounds good, Joe," I said. "I'll see you then."

I'm starting to think of favorite memories now, my own Top 40 Moments of Life. Tonight, when I saw the hazy sky just before sunset—at that magic moment when everything is in suspended animation—I remembered the evening when Rose and I sat at the back of the yard in the fairy circle of cottonwood trees. We watched our neighbors' horses run wild, back and forth in the pasture, ghostlike, kicking up dust and surrounding themselves with halos of sunshine and dirt as they snorted and stomped.

Rose sat quietly, mesmerized by their power. Then she took my hand and whispered, "Mommy, are they real?" At that moment, I couldn't say for sure.

My heart aches when I think about this, not just because I miss Rose, but because I miss myself. Where was I in all those moments, and why did I think they weren't enough?

I think about that sound—the sound of the clattering dishes—that marked the moment of "I'm done." Today I stopped by Rosa's for a late lunch, and I listened to all the chatter around me. This time it sounded like the humming of life, like comforting energy. So what is it? Why did I loathe this sound three weeks ago and decide it signaled the end of my life, while today I wanted to sit in it and breathe it in like oxygen?

I'm still anxious about the process of death—will I experience any pain? Will I suffer? But I'm no longer fearful of life. I suppose because I know I may not be here much longer, and nothing can touch me. I have become like walking Teflon. Before, death represented the ultimate fear. But with that Big One marked off the list, everything else seems like a cartoon-character villain. Disappointing someone? Piece of cake. Missing a deadline? Not a problem. Not that I want to be irresponsible or insensitive, even now. In fact, it's the opposite. I can see what I did to myself with all those pressures and fears, and I want to say to everyone I meet, "Let yourself off the hook. Turn off the murder investigation shows and the political hotheads and reality TV and go take a walk and look at the sky. Trust that you'll be okay, because you will."

It's like the e-mail that keeps circulating on the Internet— the one about how, at the end of your life, you won't care if you kept your house spotless. Instead, you'll care whether you went to your kids' soccer games and said, "I love you" every day. Turns out, that e-mail is right, but it's so much more than that. I guess that's why those things sometimes seem so simple. Because to try to put in words how profound they are would be impossible. It's like trying to describe a Minnesota lake when the glow of the moon turns the water to gold. You just can't imagine how beautiful it is until you're there.

I've been lying awake at night thinking about where I might be in a few days. If the pearls are still potent, what will the end of this life mean? What will the transition be like? Where will I be?

When Rose died, I longed to see or understand where

she was. I suppose it's the maternal instinct. You want to know where your child is and that she's okay. And even though I wanted to believe that the arms of a greater being held her safe—safer than she could ever be here on Earth—I still wanted to see her, to know what existence looked like for her.

So I lay down and closed my eyes and asked for vision, to be given the gift of knowing where she is. I saw white buildings, magnificent white buildings with columns and Greek statues. Waterfalls and fountains and gardens. I didn't see a street paved with gold or a choir of angels with harps. But I knew that exquisite beauty surrounded her.

I saw her there sitting on the steps of one of those buildings, smiling at me, and I had the sense that she's okay and happy. And that the thing she wants most for me is to be happy, too. I wish I knew how. I really do. I don't want to disappoint her. I don't know what she might think of my taking the pearls. I guess I may find out soon. There is a part of me that worries I may end up in a different place since I've taken the path of accelerated decline. But all I can do is hope that my motives will be taken into account: that all I want is to be with Mama and my little girl again.

I've been getting e-mails and Facebook messages from some of the people who received the recycled Christmas cards I sent a few days ago. My favorite came from Ardis Fletcher, a nurse who took care of Rose in the hospital after the accident.

I saw on Facebook that she's still at the hospital, but no longer in the pediatric ICU. Now she's the head of nursing for the pediatric oncology unit. She's a big, no-nonsense, nurturing kind of soul who never kowtowed to the doctors, never patronized us, and made us feel like Rose was her only patient. She was part nurse, part chaplain, part shaman. Exactly the kind of person you need in your life in a time of trauma. She'd served in the military, so she knew trauma from all sides.

She knew that healing is 10 percent physical and 90 percent everything else. I always felt that she knew from the beginning Rose wasn't going to make it. She gave Rose every chance she could, but she also helped start the healing process for us. We were every bit as much her patients as Rose.

Dear Meg, she wrote. *You made my day with the Christmas card. I'd forgotten all about sending that card to you and your family so many years ago.*

I'm not supposed to have favorite patients, of course, just like a mom isn't supposed to favor any of her kids. But you and Rose and your family left a deep impression on me. I remember Rose telling me that she worried about her horse, and how she didn't want him to feel bad. That kind of empathy is the reason I love working with little ones. I learn so much from them every day.

Thank you for being part of my family. I hope you're doing well and enjoying Christmas in August!

As I had with Holly and the trip to Seattle, I knew all of a sudden I needed to go see her. That's one of the things that's changing. Before, I would have put it on my to-do list, and I might have gotten around to it months from now. Today, when I get a nudge, I act.

I took a chance and drove the forty-five minutes to the hospital, hoping I could see Ardis for just a minute. If not, I had flowers for her—a small bouquet since I had to search the garden for flowers that looked good enough to cut. I had another card, too, and a donation to the hospital that I wanted to deliver into her hands.

I saw her right away, by the nurses' station. She hasn't changed much. She still carries herself with that regal, in-charge bearing, but manages to befriend everyone around her.

I was surprised that she knew me right away. "Meg!" she said, putting down a chart and coming to swallow me and the bouquet of flowers in those big arms of hers. "You came! How did you know I wanted to say thank you for the Christmas card in person?"

I smiled and felt the familiarity of her hug, like sitting in the crook of a wise old tree. How *did* I know?

"You haven't changed a bit," she said. "Whatever you're doing, keep doing it."

"It's so good to see you," I said. "I wanted to bring you these." I handed the flowers to her.

"What?" She held the vase out in front of her like the Olympic flame. "How thoughtful. Are these from your garden?"

"Yes," I said, shocked by her memory. "How could you possibly remember that I garden?"

"Are you kidding?" she said, waving me into her office. "You and your mom knew more about gardens than anyone I've ever met.

"Here, sit down," she said, then cleared a spot on her desk for the bouquet.

"I remember all the flowers in Rose's room," she said. "I didn't know the names of half of them, but you and your mom were like encyclopedias. What they were, what kind of growing conditions they needed, when they bloomed. How is your mom, by the way?"

I rearranged myself in the chair. "She passed away five years ago," I said.

Ardis leaned forward and murmured, "I'm so sorry. So sorry."

"She had dementia and was declining," I said, "and then she took a fall. She died not long after that. But she died at home. I was able to be with her even at the very end."

"My, my," Ardis said, her voice lower and more resonant. "You've really been through it, haven't you?" Her sympathy came over me like a wave and filled every pore, like being comforted by your mother when you're a child. My tears took me by surprise.

"She was a great woman. I only knew her those couple of days you all were here, but I could see what an elegant and gracious person she was. You must miss her terribly. Her and Rose. Are you doing okay? Getting along okay without them? You never stop missing them, do you?"

"It's been hard," I said. "But I'm getting along."

She handed me a box of tissues. "I get it," she said. "Grief never really goes away. And sometimes it sneaks up on you when you think you've got it all under control."

I felt embarrassed. This wasn't why I'd come to see her. But I sat silent for a moment, unable to talk.

"I just wanted to say thank you," I said finally, turning the tissue over and over in my hands. "You did more for us in those couple of days than you'll ever know."

"It was an honor to be with you and your family," she said. "I see a lot of heartbreaking situations in my job, and the saddest ones are when there's no closeness, when people have walled off the love. That's one of the reasons I remember you and your family so well. You were all so tender with each other. I don't see that every day."

All of a sudden, I felt as if I shared her mind, remembering the same scene she was picturing from sixteen years ago.

Joe and I sat in the ICU waiting room. Rose was asleep, and Mama had gone to the cafeteria to get something to eat. I was curled up in the crook of Joe's arm, and he was stroking my hair. Still connected. Before we shattered apart. Ardis walked into the waiting room to give us an update on Rose's medication, and I saw her looking at us for a moment before she spoke, as if she didn't want to interrupt the intimacy of the moment.

I came back to my own mind again, looking at Ardis

across the desk, as though we both exited the memory at the same time. I saw her glancing at my naked ring finger. She didn't say anything.

"Well, I don't want to keep you," I said, suddenly eager to leave. "I just wanted to stop by and give you the flowers and this." I pulled the envelope with the check from my purse and laid it on her desk next to the flowers. "It's for the hospital, but I wanted to deliver it to you."

I stood up, not wanting to remember anything else that might turn me inside out from weeping. She stood, too, and came around the desk to give me another hug.

"Thank you for coming, Meg," she said, sensitive to my vulnerability. "You take care of yourself, okay?"

"I will," I said. "Thank you, Ardis."

"Hope to see you again sometime soon," she said. I looked at her one last time before I left her office, realizing my grief had not subsided one bit since I'd seen her sixteen years before.

Suddenly I had an overwhelming desire to see Joe.

DAY FIFTEEN

Making amends always makes me think of amending soil in a garden. You start with depleted soil that's lost all its nutrients. It can't feed the plants, can't help hydrate roots, is devoid of life-giving organisms and earthworms. And so you amend it with compost. You dig in and add black, rich compost to the soil. You make it nutritive again. Sustaining. Nourishing.

Sometimes I think people look at making amends as asking for forgiveness. I guess it can be that, too. But I've always thought of mending relationships as adding some good compost and seeing them come back to life again.

Maybe, after today, that's possible with Joe.

I hadn't been to Lulu's for years, and it hadn't changed. Same slick red vinyl booths, same big retro clock over the soda fountain. I got there a few minutes before noon, wanting to be the first to arrive. I hadn't seen Joe since Mama's funeral.

I wanted to see him walking along the street and get a glimpse of him so I could set my expression straight before he walked in and saw what I was feeling. And I did. I saw him crossing the street and walking in the door. He hadn't changed much. Same sandy brown hair, although it's a little thinner on top. Same blue eyes. Same scar on one cheek from a fight with one of his brothers when he was twelve years old.

I wasn't prepared for how I felt when I saw him. Maybe knowing this could be the last time opened up a door in me that I'd shut a long time ago.

When he saw me, he waved, and his whole face seemed to smile. He came over to the booth and instead of sliding into his seat, he took my hands, pulled me up, and hugged me.

"It's so good to see you, Meg," he said. "You look younger than ever." Why did people keep saying that?

"You look good, too," I said as he sat down and pushed the catsup and mustard rack over to the side of the table, out of our way.

"Thank you for coming to meet me," he said. "This must be a hard time for you."

For a moment I wondered if he somehow knew about the pearls. We'd always had a special connection. But there was no way he could know.

"It's hard to believe it's been five years since your mom left us," he said. *Oh yes, Mama's death.*

I fidgeted with the paper place mat on the table. "I'm getting along okay," I said. "How about you? How's the conference going?"

"Good," he said. "I'm glad we could get together. It's been too long, and I thought it might be a comfort to you, seeing an old familiar face about now."

Again, it seemed he knew more than he said.

"Did you move?" I asked. "I noticed you had a new return address on the card you sent." I tried to pretend I didn't know, that Holly and Phil hadn't told me about his divorce.

He looked down at the table. "Well," he said. "There have been some changes in my life. Carol and I aren't together anymore."

I tried not to show that I already knew. "What happened?" I asked. "Well, not that it's any of my business."

"We'd been having problems for a while," he said. He rubbed his ring finger. "It always seemed as if our relationship was missing something, and we finally agreed that it just wasn't working."

"I'm so sorry," I said, partly meaning it.

"We're still friends," he said. "I still get together with the girls. . . . I think it helps them to have a second dad in their lives."

"I'm sure," I said. "You were always a terrific dad."

He smiled and looked at me. "Thank you," he said.

The waitress came and took our order.

"So, tell me what you've been up to," he said. I'd been rehearsing how I would answer this question. I had a cheerful stock response for acquaintances I ran into. But not for Joe.

"Oh, the same old thing. Trying to survive the heat, like everybody."

"Are the plants surviving?"

"Barely," I said. "I water them four times a day, and they still look stressed. They need what I can't give them." I didn't say I felt the same way.

"How are things at Nancy's?"

"Slow," I said. "I'm taking a couple of weeks off. I figured it would help Nancy if she didn't have to pay me, and the break is giving me a chance to catch up on a few things." A part of me wanted to tell him what I'd done, blurt out the whole story, but I pretended to read the menu instead.

"Anything that needs fixing?" he said. "I'll be around

for a few days. I'd be happy to come out and help you if you need something. It would be great to spend some time at the old place again."

My stomach turned. The thought of him back at the acreage, back at the same place where we found Rose in the pasture with Romeo pawing the ground, with all those memories, made me want to throw up and gave me a strange sense of elation at the same time.

"Really, Meg," he said, "if you need anything at all, I'd like to help."

I felt the familiarity of his offer. Genuine, no hidden agenda. The guy I could always count on, being steadfast once again.

"I'll give it some thought," I said. "You know how things are at the farm. There's always something that needs repair."

When we walked out of the diner and into the heat, it felt as if we were walking into a furnace. Without any breeze, the heat hung over the street, completely still. Joe gave me a proper hug.

"I'll call you tonight and see if you need me the next couple of days," he said. "I'll be free tomorrow after five. . . . I could bring supper out if you like."

I nodded. "Thanks, Joe," I said. "I'll talk to you later." And then he was gone.

I stopped on the way home and bought a red dress, which I realized made about as much sense as scheduling a teeth cleaning next month or having the oil changed in the car. What possessed me, I wasn't sure, but since I seemed to be following my intuition rather than logic, I gave in to the urge.

At the boutique, Jennifer asked me if had a special occasion coming up. Why had I even gone into the store, any-way? And what could I say in answer to her question? I've known Jen for years. She brought manicotti to the house after Rose died, and she stopped by a couple of times with sweaters that she thought Mama would like.

"No big occasion," I said, thumbing through the sale rack.

"Damn," she said, "I thought maybe you had some news."

I smiled. "I can always pretend," I said.

"I've got something I think would look great on you," she said, headed to a rack of new arrivals.

When she held the dress up to me and had me look in the mirror, I couldn't help myself. I had to try it on. It looked like something I would have chosen for a date night with Joe, with a flouncy skirt and a jewel neckline. It might just hang in my closet, unworn. But I think it would fit Holly, so it won't go to waste. And it makes me happy. One final indulgence.

I hung it on the outside of the bedroom closet door where I can see it. And then I dug through the rest of my closet and filled two garbage bags with clothes that I'll take to Goodwill tomorrow. If I'm actually going Home, I want the last things I see in this house to be things I love.

I checked the mail as soon as I got home. Still no lab results. For some reason I remembered that church sign, WE LOVE HURTING PEOPLE, and I laughed out loud even while I crumpled into a heap next to the mailbox.

"I'm so sorry," Carla said when I called. "I'll have the lab put another copy of the results in the mail to you."

I thought about saying, "Don't bother. It's too late." But instead I thanked her and sat staring at the colored swirls on the wall.

* * *

I went for a walk in the hills this evening, and for the first time ever, I didn't waste time wondering how many calories I was burning or whether my thighs would look slimmer in the morning. Those things seem irrelevant now. Have they always been?

It surprised me to see what I noticed along the way. There was life in the woods, even under all the dryness from the drought. I saw a kind of wildflower I'd never noticed before and three rocks that looked like the sky. I sat by the pond for a few minutes, where Mama and I scattered Cricket's ashes after he died, and a group of swallows flew over it, swooping and curving, as graceful as ballerinas.

I try to imagine what life will be like on the other side, and that's how I think it might be—beauty and peace magnified one thousand times over. I feel as if I'm going on a secret vacation, savoring it all myself.

But clearly there's more beauty right here in front of me than I've ever seen before. I realize how many things have passed me by because I felt too afraid to look, or I didn't take the time to look, or I was too angry to look. When I ceased to matter as a mother, a wife, and a daughter, I forgot that I matter simply as a human being.

One winter years ago, when Rose was about eight, she carefully sculpted a spider out of snow. It had a big mound for its body, surrounded by eight long legs. Joe and I had just come outside to take a picture when Cricket got excited, ran around in circles, and jumped right on top of it.

"Cricket!" Rose yelled. "Get off of there!" Too late. The whole thing collapsed into just another pile of snow.

I grabbed Cricket by the collar and made him sit. Joe walked over to Rose and put his arm around her, surveying the damage.

"I'm sorry that happened," he said.

"You and me both," she said, kicking at the snow with

her boot. "I worked on that all day. It was the best thing I've ever made." She was not above exaggeration.

"Looks like you have two choices," Joe said. "You can be mad, or you can have fun building it all over again. Which sounds better to you?"

Rose thought for a moment, then looked up at her dad and squinted in the sun.

"Wanna help me?" she asked.

The photo of Rose with her bigger-and-better snow spider became one of Joe's favorites. He carried it around in his wallet for years. For all I know, it's still there.

DAY SIXTEEN

I was just finishing breakfast this morning when I heard a car in the driveway. It was Miriam, stopping by on her way to work.

"Hey, you," I said as she came up on the porch. "Thank you for taking care of the plants while I was away."

"Don't mention it," she said, waving her hand as though she were shooing away a bug.

"How was your time with the kids?" I asked.

She rolled her eyes. "I'll tell you when the credit card bills come in," she said. "I thought *dorm* rooms were expensive. Do you have any idea how much money it takes to outfit rooms in a sorority and fraternity? Not to mention all the clothes. Good lord."

No, I don't have any idea, I thought. Once upon a time, her words would have stung. I was surprised that I took no offense at them.

"I want to hear all about your trip," she said, "but I'm running late for my first appointment. I just wanted to drop this by."

She pulled an envelope out of her purse.

The lab results.

I could see the health clinic's logo in the corner.

"It got delivered to my address by mistake," she said. "You'd think the mailman would know better after all these years, wouldn't you?"

I stared at the envelope as though it had fallen from the sky. "Probably just got mixed up when they held the mail for both of us while we were gone."

"Well, that's a nice way of looking at it," Miriam said. "Anyway, I'm sorry I was away and couldn't get it to you before now. Hope it's not too important."

"No, don't worry," I said. "Thanks for bringing it by."

"Well, gotta run," she said, headed to her car. "Let's have another margarita night soon so I can hear about Holly and her family. And don't forget about those dreadlocks!" She winked and waved as she got in the car.

I won't forget, I thought, peeling back the flap on the envelope. *I will remember every moment.*

When Rose was a toddler, she laughed a lot, and she ran figure eights around the clothesline poles over and over until she made herself dizzy and fell down. Cricket ran with her and barked, encouraging her. He slept with her, too. A big old mutt of a guy, he was twice her size and her protector from day one.

He licked her hair, right on top of her head—grooming her or creating a protective helmet. I'd comb her hair afterward to get some of the oil-slick saliva out of it, but ten minutes later, when she fell asleep on the rug on the living room floor, Cricket would come over, lick her head a couple more times, then stretch out next to her in vigil.

I remember those afternoons of watching her while she played and slept, hoping one day she'd have a man as loyal as Cricket to watch over her. It wasn't that she couldn't take care of herself. But I always wanted her to be treated like the treasure she was. Appreciated and cherished.

That's one of the reasons I took the pearls, I think. Because I saw all the lack of cherishing in the world. Kids shot in their schools. Leaders of countries slaughtering their own people. Policemen ambushed and killed. Animals driven to extinction. How can we have a world without elephants or polar bears?

I took the pearls because I didn't cherish myself or anyone else. And now I see that that's the only thing we're here to do. Really. The only thing.

So that's why I did something today that I thought I would never do. I called the monastery, the one where I went to the grief retreat and wrote my letters to God. The letters have been sitting in my bedroom the last few days, on top of the last box of old shoes and clothes slated for Goodwill. I couldn't bring myself to throw them away, or even to look at them. Too much pain. But I don't have years to wonder what to do with them or delay a decision or bury them back in the closet.

So I picked up the phone and dialed.

"Father Xavier, please," I said, unsure whether he was still alive.

"I'm sorry," a peaceful male voice on the other end said. "Father Xavier is infirm and unable to speak with anyone right now. Can someone else help you?"

"Yes," I said, surprisingly confident. "I think I need to talk to a priest. I came to a retreat with Father Xavier many years ago, but maybe I could talk with someone else?"

"I'm sorry he's not available," the voice said. "But I could certainly talk with you. I'm Father David. Are you able to come here in person?"

I took a deep breath and said, "Yes. Could I see you tomorrow?"

He must have heard the clarity in my voice.

"Certainly," he said. "Would one p.m. work?"

"Yes, thank you." That would give me time to make the two-hour drive.

"Very well," he said calmly, touching a place of peace in me. "Do you know how to find us?"

"Yes," I said, "I remember."

"Fine," he said. "I'll see you tomorrow afternoon."

There's a lot in this house that needs fixing. Mama always kept it so neat and fresh, always in good repair. But I just haven't had the energy.

Two of the tiles over the bathtub are broken. The wallpaper in the dining room is starting to peel. One of the windows in the living room is cracked. The barn is sagging a bit and looks weathered. And I never patched the bathroom ceiling after it had water damage from the leak in the attic last year.

I could have had someone come in for repairs, but it never seemed to be a priority. Now that there is less clutter, it's easier to see what needs work.

I felt a little embarrassed to have Joe see it this way. I could hide the cracks in myself, but not in the plaster. All the imperfections would be in full view. But I was tired of hiding. I wondered what it would feel like to have him back in the house again. The first time since our divorce.

He came over late this afternoon. I could smell the dust from the gravel road even before I heard his car. He parked near the shed and stepped out into the same driveway, with the same beds of flowers blooming in the background.

How could everything and nothing change at the same time?

He wore a white polo shirt and khaki pants, and he carried a bag of tacos—the fry-bread tacos we both loved.

"Hey, you're too dressed up to do any work around this place," I said. He reached out and gave me a quick hug.

"Not to worry," he said. "I've got jeans and a T-shirt in the back. Thought I'd size things up first."

"Well, come on in out of the heat," I said.

He stood for a moment and turned in a circle, taking it all in. I tried to see the place through his eyes. Fourteen years.

"I'd forgotten how beautiful it is," he said, surveying the hills in the distance. "You probably never get tired of it."

"Sometimes," I said. "You know how it is. You take things for granted after a while."

He nodded and looked off toward the shed and the barn. "The flowers are looking good," he said. "Your mom would be proud."

They looked stronger and healthier than they had in weeks. The hosta blooms in the memorial garden stood straight and tall. I could feel vitality and aliveness from them again. Would the powder from Lin Chow have had the same effect on me?

"Thanks. It's been a challenge this summer. The drought has taken its toll."

"Well," he said, "you must be doing something right, because I certainly couldn't tell."

We walked up the steps to the front porch. He stood in one spot and leaned back and forth, making one of the floorboards moan. "Same squeak," he said, smiling.

When he walked into the house, I had that sense of elation again, like giddiness to see him, to feel him once again in this house. He walked through the kitchen door, set the bag down on the kitchen table, and looked around. "It hasn't changed," he said. He rubbed his nose and then one eye—his way of holding back tears.

"No," I said. "I've kept it pretty much like Mama had it."

"Except for this," he said, zeroing in on the colors on

the wall. He seemed pleased to find something to tease me about. "What happened here?'

"Kind of crazy, huh?" I said, letting him off the hook.

"No," he said. "It reminds me of the colored lights you told me about. The ones that were there with Rose."

I didn't move. "You remember that?" I said.

"Of course." He reached out to touch the wall and feel the texture of the paint. "I remember the first time you told me about them. It was one of the things that I always loved about you and our relationship, that you'd trust me enough to tell me things that other people didn't know or understand about you. And I always felt that you were connected to something I wish I could be connected to. I've thought about that a lot the past few years. It's always inspired me."

Inspired him.

Next to my sister, he's the person on this planet who has known me the longest. And in many ways, he knows me more intimately than my own sister does.

"I got a wild hair the other day," I said, handing him some plates from the cupboard for our meal. "I found some old paint in the shed and something just came over me."

"Ah, the shed," he said. "I remember it well." I knew exactly what he was recalling. "We just about kicked over some of those cans of paint." He smiled.

"Is it hard living with all these memories?" he said, pulling the tacos out of the bag.

"Not really," I lied. I wanted to break down in tears, tell him how lonely I'd been, how I felt I'd been living with ghosts and didn't see the point anymore, but I didn't. "I guess I like the old and familiar."

"That's me," he said. "Old and familiar."

We both laughed.

"Want some iced tea?" I asked.

We sat down to eat. "Help yourself," I said, handing him the platter of tacos.

"Thanks," he said. He paused. "Do you mind if I get something off my chest?" he said. I stiffened, wondering what was to come.

He took a sip of his tea and looked at me.

"I never told you how much I blamed myself for leaving," he said.

I breathed deeply, as though inhaling his words. I felt a boulder roll away from my heart, revealing an entrance.

"I never blamed you," I said. "I blamed myself. I pushed you away, even when I didn't want to."

"But I should have stayed," he said. "I could see what you were doing, what I was doing. I just thought that maybe if I left, things would right themselves again somehow, and it would just be temporary. I never meant to stay away."

I remembered the day he left, seeing the light go out of his eyes. Aside from losing Rose, I've never experienced anything more painful.

"Do you remember what you said to me when you left that day?" I asked.

"Yes," he said. "'I hope you find what you're looking for.' I meant it for myself, too."

"You did, you moved on. You found Carol and the girls. I thought you were happy."

"There were moments of happiness—definitely," he said. "But it always felt like something important was missing, like we were trying to fill some gaping hole. And no matter how hard we tried, the hole didn't go away."

"And what was it?" I asked, feeling my heart soften a little more.

"History," he said. "Some deeper connection and understanding. You and I always had it. We just knew each other from the start. With Carol, it seemed we were always acquaintances looking for something more."

I could hear myself breathing. "We did have something special," I said.

"Yes, we did," he said. "And I miss it. We were part of each other. We still are."

All of a sudden I remembered the pearls. I'd been so involved in the conversation that I'd forgotten. He'd taken me away from it, just like he always did. And now I didn't know what to say.

"So what do you want?" I asked.

"To spend time with you," he said. "To be friends again. To see if we can create a new relationship with each other."

I sat back in my chair and looked at him, feeling deeply sorrowful for what I'd done. He was offering me a new chance. And under other circumstances, I would have taken it.

"I don't know," I said. "I want to, but there are circumstances. . . ."

"Are you seeing someone else?" he asked.

"God, no," I said. "Honestly, I haven't been interested. Not really. I know what you're saying about Carol. That's how I've felt about other men."

"Then what is it?"

"I wish I could tell you," I said. "Let's give it a few days—let me think about it."

"Okay," he said slowly, trying to understand. "I'll accept that. In the meantime, do you mind if I hang around when I can? I don't have to be back in California until next week."

I froze, not sure what to do. And then I felt the boulder rolling away from the cave again, as if both of us had been resurrected, and I said yes. I'm not sure how, but no matter what happens four days from now, I feel better knowing he's nearby.

His whole body seemed to relax. He sat back in his chair. "Good," he said, with the same smile I remember from years ago. He lifted his taco in the air. "To new beginnings," he said.

When I opened the lab results this morning, I sat for the longest time and stared at them on the kitchen table, rereading every number. Normal. Normal. Normal. The only note from my doctor was a reminder to schedule a routine mammogram and colonoscopy.

So I know nothing more than before. Nothing to help me prepare or resist. Nothing to do but wait, and I am so tired of waiting.

I did learn one thing. If I'm still here August 29, I'll start a new to-do list with this as my first resolution: *Be in the moment.* As Joe wrote on my list a long time ago, *Breathe in. Breathe out.*

And if I don't live on? I worry about the death being painful, but Dr. Edelman said it would be peaceful. Maybe no different from walking from one room into another. In many ways, I've been crossing new thresholds already, letting go of everything that didn't work for me, which means I'm getting healthier. How ironic is that? And the fact that now I see what life could be yet won't be here to live it creates a deep anger. It looks like I've cheated myself once more.

Joe never did anything wrong in our marriage. The only thing I couldn't forgive him for was that he wanted to go on living after Rose died, and I didn't. I needed to grieve. He did, too, but he always said that Rose would have wanted us to go on with life, to enjoy it the way she did. She wouldn't want us to be stuck in our grief, and so he moved on. And I couldn't forgive him for that. How could he keep going when the world had stopped?

The thing about grief is that you can't turn it off—or even turn it down. It's like a flame that just keeps burning, a slow and corrosive anger at yourself and God and nature itself. I didn't grow any flowers for two years after she died. It seemed irrelevant to me. Everything did, including my marriage. So I've never really blamed Joe for leaving. How could he live with a person who was dead inside?

After dinner tonight, Joe helped me wash the dishes. We did them by hand, the way we used to. Then we took our iced tea out to the porch and sat on the swing, where a bit of a breeze rustled the crisp leaves on the trees.

"You've got cats?" Joe said, noticing the bowl of food.

"A barn cat and two of her kittens," I said. "There were four, but I think coyotes got the other two."

"I'm sorry," Joe said. "Have you tried calling them in your mind? You always had that connection with nature. Why don't you try it?"

There he was again, reminding me of parts of myself that I'd dismissed long ago, that have been so covered up by guilt and regret that I've forgotten my own essential nature.

He looked out over the hills and said, "I know you were angry at me for not grieving the way you were grieving. I can see now that you thought I didn't care as much as you did, that I didn't miss Rose as much. That wasn't true, but I just didn't know how to show it without losing my mind."

I took in a big breath. This sounded honest and right.

"I was scared, Meg. I was afraid that if I felt anything, my whole world would spin out of control. I just kept putting one foot in front of the other, trying to go on. I can see now how that must have looked to you. But losing Rose, and then losing you—life hasn't been the same since. There just hasn't been any joy in it for me."

I sat still, stunned. He was describing the same thing I've felt.

"I just wanted to see you and tell you I'm sorry."

"You don't need to be sorry about anything," I said. "I pushed you away." I tensed my body, willing myself to stay under control, when I just wanted to put my head on his shoulder and weep for all the years I'd missed him, and for the decision I'd made. How could I tell him I'd be gone in four days? And how do I know whether that's even true?

We sat in silence for a few minutes, watching the sun sink in the sky. The crickets started chirping, a few lightning bugs came out, and the haze over the hills became thicker, blurring the sun.

"Well," he said, "I guess I'd better be going. The conference starts early in the morning."

My heart hurt to think of him leaving and the house being empty again.

"Do you mind if I call you tomorrow?" he said. "I didn't get anything fixed for you tonight. . . . Maybe you'll give me another chance?"

I remembered my appointment with Father David. "How about Friday?" I said. "I'm making a little day trip tomorrow."

He smiled and nodded. "Sure," he said. "Day after tomorrow then."

"Just bring steaks next time," I said.

"That's a deal," he said. He stood up, offered me his hand, and I got up and walked with him into the kitchen and put the glasses in the sink. "It's good seeing you, Joe," I said.

"You too, Meg," he said, and kissed me on the cheek. I watched him drive away, the dust from the road gathering in a cloud behind him. For just a moment, I forgot the deadline looming ahead of me and, for the first time in years, felt what could only be described as joy.

DAY SEVENTEEN

I wrapped a new rubber band around the bundle of letters I'd written at the monastery after Rose died. I slid them into a big envelope, then set them on the passenger seat next to me. I wasn't sure what I'd do with them when I got to the monastery, or what I'd say to Father David, but something compelled me to take them along. I tucked a sandwich in a bag to eat along the way and set out.

As I got closer, off the main highway and onto the gravel road leading back to the monastery, I felt prickly, as though all the pain of sixteen years ago had come back and crawled under my skin. The monastery was lovely, really, built of limestone and sitting on top of a hill, surrounded by farm fields. But it looked threatening, like someone who knew the worst part of who I was. I had to force myself to park the car and walk inside rather than turning around and driving back home.

Funny what deadlines will make you do.

I walked into the foyer and saw the chapel off to the left. I remembered it well. The place where I sat and heard other grieving people open up their hearts and spill their pain all over us. I didn't want to be that broken or needy, but I was.

A priest with thinning brown hair and glasses stood behind the reception desk. His plain white robe matched the simplicity of the crucifix that hung on the wall behind him.

"I'm Father David," he said. "Are you Meg?"

I nodded and stuck out my hand, unsure how to greet a priest. He took my hand in both of his and said, "I'm glad you've come. Let's find a place where we can sit in private."

He led me down the beige halls to a small room with a big oak table and several swivel chairs. I remembered that the priests held twelve-step recovery retreats here and wondered how many people had sat in these chairs to make amends of their own.

"Now," he said, "how can I help you?"

I laid the envelope on the table as if it were a bomb about to explode.

"Well," I said, "as I mentioned on the phone, I came here for a grief retreat sixteen years ago. My ten-year-old daughter had died recently, and I was very angry."

Father David nodded slightly, encouraging me to go on.

"Father Xavier suggested that I write letters to God, expressing my pain. I did, and I've never looked at them again before now. I feel a need to talk about what's in them. I think maybe if I do, something in me will be healed. I don't know. I hope so."

"I hope so, too," Father David said. "I'm happy to be a witness for you."

He moved a box of tissues closer to me on the table. I could feel the tears coming already, like a tide I couldn't stop. How could there still be this much pain after all these years?

"Would you be willing to read the letters to me?" he asked.

"Read them?" I said, taken by surprise. "Out loud?" The thought of talking about them at all challenged me enough. But to say the words in those letters in this room, in front of this stranger . . . I might as well stand naked and beat myself with a stick.

"Yes," he said. "I know it may be painful, but reading the letters will bring you face-to-face with them. That's the best way for healing to take place."

I sat and stared at the letters, waiting for the bomb to explode. I had given them all my power. I'd poured myself into them and then locked them up in the back of the closet all those years ago. Father David was right. I had to face them.

I nodded, surrendering to the pain. He made me feel safe. I trusted his guidance. Ironic, really, considering that the same kind of trust had led me to write the letters in the first place.

"May I say a prayer before you read the letters?" he asked.

"Yes," I said. "Although I want you to know that I'm not Catholic. I'm not anything, really. I hope that's okay. "

"Certainly," he said. "You're a child of God. We are all part of His family."

He closed his eyes and said, "Heavenly Father, we ask for Your blessings on Meg as she seeks to restore her relationship with You. Please be with us both in this sacred time of healing. In the name of the Father, the Son, and the Holy Ghost." He made the sign of the cross and opened his eyes.

"Now," he said, "whenever you're ready."

I took a tissue from the box and set it in my lap, then slowly slid the letters out of the envelope. I unfolded the first one, took a deep breath, and began to read.

"Dear God," I read. *"I am destroyed. My little girl is gone, and You have given me no comfort of any kind. How could You let this happen? How could You watch while, in one moment, I lost the most precious thing in the world? How could You cut short a life with so much*

beauty and potential? How could You rob Rose and all of us of the life we could have had? Should have had.

"We did nothing wrong. Nothing to deserve this. And now it's irreparable. You've pulled up everything beautiful and blooming by the roots and thrown it on the ground as if You don't care. You never cared.

"You took my father when I was a child, and now You've taken my child.

"'The Lord is my shepherd; I shall not want. He maketh me to lie down in green pastures; he leadeth me beside the still waters.' You talked about the peace which passeth all understanding, and I believed You.

"I didn't know until now that God is a vicious liar."

I stopped and looked at Father David, wondering if I'd crossed a line.

He showed no judgment or condemnation. "Go on," he said calmly. "This takes great courage."

I continued reading, stopping every minute or two to blow my nose and wipe my eyes, wishing I felt brave. Instead I felt defiant and destroyed all over again. Every single bit of pain resurfaced within me.

The pain had been dormant. I'd made it dormant. But like an invasive plant, it had taken over more of me than I'd realized. It put down deep roots underground and spread, just waiting for the chance to assert itself and take over.

How could I not have healed at all in these sixteen years? I remembered the woman in the grief group that I hadn't wanted to be. At least she'd admitted that the wound hadn't healed, that it was still as raw and gaping and fresh as ever.

I'd pretended all these years. Held it in, pushed Joe away, poured myself into Mama, and lost myself right along with her. No wonder I'd taken the pearls. There was nothing to kill.

I'd forgotten how hateful the letters were. Like pure venom. Anger directed at everyone, but mostly against myself. When I came to the words I'd forgotten I'd written, the ones I've never said out loud to anyone, I could feel the acid in my mouth as I read them.

But as I read, I felt some glimmer in me coming back, as though a flame that had been lying in embers all these years received a puff of oxygen and sprang to life again. I read for most of an hour, stopping frequently to sit and weep.

Father David never changed his demeanor. Stoic, but kind. Simply witnessing. He gave me a human form for God so I could have my say and feel heard at last. He allowed me to pull up all the invasive weeds by the roots and get them outside of me, putting an end to their destructive power.

Finally I finished the last letter. I blew my nose again and looked at Father David, my eyes red and throbbing.

"You are very brave," he said simply. And then he said something unexpected.

"Would you like to burn the letters?"

I felt a little leap in my heart, as though that long-ignored flame received another puff of air.

"Yes, please," I said.

Father David led me outside behind the monastery to a large outdoor fireplace built from the same limestone as the building. I stood and looked around, taking in the fragrance of freshly cut grass and the majesty of evergreen trees, their rich color silhouetted against the blue sky.

In the distance, two monks with baskets gathered produce from neat vegetable gardens. Even though they were far away, I could see the deep reds and greens of the tomatoes and zucchini, and I could feel the respect the men had for their harvest. It seemed as though the drought had affected everything in the state but this single patch of land.

"We'll keep the fire small," Father David said, bringing

my attention back to the letters. "No more than we need." He placed some kindling in the fireplace and lit it with a match.

"Add the letters carefully," he said. I breathed deeply, trying to steady myself. Then I took them one by one, unfolded them again, and placed them on the pyre of kindling.

Father David and I were silent as I added each letter, placing it solemnly, like flowers on a grave. And when all of the letters were on the fire, we stood in silence for several more minutes.

I watched the edges of the paper crinkle and blacken and curl as the words melted into the paper and disappeared. Bits of ash floated into the air, carrying my anger and bitterness into the heat of the day.

I felt exhausted but cleansed. It reminded me of my confirmation when I was little, a ceremony that had little meaning for me at the time, but did make me feel as if something new had happened. I remember when the pastor touched me on the head. I felt a bolt of energy travel down my spine and settle in my gut, as though a seed had been planted.

Reading and burning the letters made me feel that finally, maybe, that seed could grow.

Three more days. Or maybe years. How much time did that seed need? How much time would it have?

Father David looked at me for a sign, and I nodded. He poured water from a coffee can on the fire until the sizzling stopped, and all was quiet.

"May I be of more help?" he asked as we walked back to the reception area. I looked toward the sanctuary and saw candles burning there.

"Is it all right if I take a moment?" I asked.

"Certainly," he said. We walked into the limestone room that had been so forbidding years ago. Light flooded

through the rows of arched windows, glancing off the tile
floor and polished pews. I made my way to a simple table
of votives and looked up at the statue of Jesus. Everything
seemed new to me. Had I seen any of this beauty sixteen
years ago?

I lit a candle for Mama, and then one for Rose, feeling
that seed in me expand and grow.

"Would you like to light a candle for your father, too?"
Father David asked.

"For God?" I said, curious.

"No." He smiled. "For your earthly father."

"Oh, yes," I said, embarrassed that I would forget about
Daddy.

I felt a peace settle over me as I lit a third votive, then
stood in silence, asking for healing of my body and soul,
not even knowing what that meant. When I opened my
eyes, I saw a shaft of sunlight streaming through one of
the high windows.

Father David stood patiently a few feet away, respecting
my privacy and the intimacy of the moment. I hadn't been
sure about coming here, but now I wasn't ready to leave.
If I could receive so much peace from facing the letters,
maybe I needed to face the pearls, as well.

"Father David," I said, lifting my face to feel the warmth
of the sun, "do you have a few more minutes? There's
something else I'd like to talk about."

DAY EIGHTEEN

Telling Father David about the pearls yesterday felt surprisingly easy after reading him the letters. It was like talking about someone else without any guilt or judgment. Just reporting what I'd done with no apology. I felt liberated, almost detached. I've always reserved that kind of compassion for others, not for myself.

Father David didn't condemn me. He didn't really even comment. No look of shock in his eyes. I don't know if he trained to be nonreactive or if he comes by it naturally. It's as though he's risen above all the things we judge ourselves and one another for, as though he's seeing something I can't.

"There are times when I've felt sinful," I told him. We sat in one of the pews, near the candles I'd lit. "Suicide is a sin, isn't it?" I asked. "But this doesn't feel like suicide. And, honestly, I don't even know what will happen. The pearls may not work at all. I was just desperate and lonely. I can see now how lonely I was."

The sun cast long rays of light through the windows, illuminating the milky creaminess of the limestone. I felt I could see every grain of sand in them, every crevice and mark of stress, every ancient scar, all creating something beautiful and whole.

He leaned toward me and put his hand on my shoulder. I knew he couldn't approve of my decision to take the pearls, but I sensed no disapproval. In fact, it seemed that he understood. That maybe he knew what loneliness was. Maybe he, too, had longed to go Home.

"You are absolved of any guilt," he said. "Whatever happens, know that you may live in peace."

That seed planted in me during my confirmation years ago broke open and sprouted, as though something new and free had finally taken root within me.

"Thank you," I said, taking one more look around the sanctuary and the candles I'd lit, still burning strong.

At the front of the sanctuary, several monks filed in and took places at the organ and along the sides of the room.

"Afternoon prayers," Father David said. "You're welcome to stay and listen."

"I appreciate that," I said, remembering the medieval-sounding chants from the grief retreat years ago. "I'd better be going, but I thank you for everything."

Father David walked with me to the front door and said good-bye, and the swelling harmony of the monks and the organ music accompanied me all the way to my car.

I sat for a moment, said the first real prayer of thanks I've said in a long time, and headed home.

Along the way, I had to stop the car twice to rest. My body felt as if someone had wrung it inside out, and I was so tired I could hardly keep my eyes on the road.

I pulled over by the side of the highway and took in the colors of the sky. With so much dust in the air, the sunsets this summer are spectacular. Who could imagine that the right combination of dirt and light could be iridescent? Like sparks of pure joy, or swirls of color dancing.

When I got home, I took a walk through the gardens to check on the flowers. Every day, it seems, they grow straighter, taller, and more vibrant.

They looked revived and rejuvenated. I marveled at their resiliency—and mine.

Then I turned down the quilt on the bed, put on my softest T-shirt, and let peace carry me into a deep sleep.

Today I cleaned all morning, going through the last junk drawers in the kitchen. Rubber bands, old keys, twist ties. All the minutiae of life that we tuck away, afraid to let go because we might need it someday.

I pulled the garbage can over to the drawers and tossed the little things by the handful, then pulled out the drawers themselves and shook them free of the crumbs and dust that had collected in the corners.

There. Another item crossed off the list. The place has come a long way in the last couple of weeks.

I watered the flowers and pulled a few weeds in the memorial garden. Then I picked a bouquet of purple asters and set them on the kitchen table, adding a splash of color as bright as the freestyle painting on the wall.

Joe came over after lunch. I heard that familiar crunching sound of the car on the gravel driveway and went out to the porch to welcome him. He carried grocery bags in both hands. "I didn't forget the steaks," he said, setting the bags on the porch swing to give me a hug.

I held the door open for him, thankful for the cool air in the kitchen. "How did your trip go yesterday?" he said, putting the steaks in the refrigerator and taking bread and salad out of the bags.

"Fine," I said, not sure how much to tell him.

"I don't mean to pry," he said, sensing my hesitation.

"No, that's okay," I said. "I'll tell you about it later."

"It's up to you," he said, turning to look me in the eye.

"I know this is sudden—our spending time together this way. You have every right to keep your life private. If you feel I'm stepping over the line, just tell me, okay?"

"Okay," I said, wanting any line between us to simply disappear.

We spent the afternoon freshening things up around the place. He found the tools in the shed and made a trip to the hardware store to get some supplies; then he started in on the pipes and the tile and the bathroom ceiling, patching things up, making the house look like someone lived here again.

I puttered in the kitchen, starting a cake for supper, marveling at the sharp sweetness of the vanilla and the texture of the coconut. Joe came in, on his way to the shed for more tools.

"Mmm," he said. "Your mom's coconut cake?"

I nodded and held out a spoon filled with batter.

"As good as ever," he said, licking it clean. He set the spoon in the sink, then turned around to look at me. "I've been meaning to ask you," he said, "do you have something big coming up this weekend?"

I felt a shiver run through me. "No. Why do you ask?"

He looked at the calendar on the wall. In all my excitement about his coming, I'd forgotten to take it down.

"Just being nosy," he said. "You've got Sunday circled, and it looks like you've been marking off some days, like you're counting down to something."

"No," I said, thinking fast. "I've been trying to lose a few pounds, and that's my deadline."

"Oh," he said, apparently satisfied. "Well, since I'm being curious, can I ask you another question?"

I froze, wondering what would come next.

"Sure," I said.

"Why did you have the mole on your face removed?"

I hadn't realized how much it was a part of me. Holly had noticed, and now Joe, too.

"Got tired of it, I guess. Didn't want it to turn into something worse. Plus, it wasn't attractive."

"I always thought it made you unique," he said. "Like your fingerprint."

Joe and I took a walk into the hills after supper when it finally started to cool down. We climbed over the barbed wire fence and walked into the Logans' hay field, the one we talked about buying back for Mama someday. That was when we looked toward expansion. A bigger family, more land, adding on, seeing the world.

From the top of the hill, we could see the pond and the valley stretching out in front of us. The cicadas were humming, a low buzz that sounded comforting and alive. I could smell the freshly cut hay, the same smell I've known since I was a baby. So much history. So much beauty. So much I've taken for granted.

Joe put his arm around my shoulder and drew me close to him, taking it all in.

"It hasn't changed much, has it?" he said.

I shook my head, listening to the quiet and remembering.

I thought back to the day of the accident. Romeo was recovering from an infection in his foot. He seemed as calm and steady as always. Joe had told Rose she couldn't ride him again until he fully healed. But he was doing so well, almost off his medication, and she begged me to let her ride him. So I did, not really thinking anything of it.

Joe came to me later and said, "We weren't going to let her ride Romeo." His voice sounded constricted, almost strangled. He'd simply made a statement, but his words pierced me as though he'd plunged a dagger right through me. My remorse immediately turned to defense.

"True," I said, feeling myself slowly turning to stone.

He said just one word: "Why?"

"Because she begged me," I said. At least that was honest.

He said nothing and walked away. I thought he had turned against me, because how could he not? I'd turned against myself.

So, tonight, out there on the hill, with his arm around me and the sky growing pink in the west and the moon coming up in the east, I asked him what I should have asked him sixteen years ago.

"How could you still want me when I killed our daughter?"

He turned, took my shoulders in his hands, and looked right into my eyes. "I never thought you killed her."

"Don't you remember the day you asked me why I let her ride Romeo? When I told you, you didn't say anything, you just walked away. I knew you were blaming me, just like I blamed myself."

Joe was quiet, his shoulders slumped. "I wasn't blaming you," he said. "I was thinking I would have done the exact same thing."

I had forgotten desire. The pilot light that burned in me all those years—even through all the miscarriages—blew out when Rose died, and it never came back. Those last years of our marriage weren't without sex, but they were without passion. And, honestly, I don't think I've ever felt it since. That lightning-fierce hunger to be touched, the primal need to be entered and known. I'd forgotten. Forgotten what it felt like. Forgotten that it mattered.

But in the last couple of days, close enough to Joe to feel his breath, to stand next to him and feel the strength of his steadiness, I began to remember. It started as a quiver inside me, much like the first fledgling wings of Rose's movements when I was four months pregnant and started to believe I wouldn't lose her like the others.

The quivers had taken root and were traveling through me, like nerve endings being fired after long dormancy, like a switchboard lighting up the night sky. A buzz. And once again, a hunger.

And then, the doubts. What if the pearls contained some sort of deadly virus and could be transmitted? What if sex after such a long abstinence was painful? What if my body couldn't consummate what my heart wanted? And, just as I feared when I was seventeen, what if I gave myself to him and he walked away? *Lord,* I thought, *doesn't that fear ever go away?*

We walked back to the house tonight in silence, but together. Together in a way we haven't been since Rose died.

When we got back inside, we stood in the kitchen with our arms around each other, and he kissed my hair and my forehead. "I'm sorry," he said.

Then he kissed me the way he always had. The way he did even after Rose died, when my body and soul went numb and couldn't return the longing.

We lost ourselves in each other slowly and patiently, remembering each other's bodies. Everything about him felt familiar. His scent, the curve of his ear, his firm but gentle grasp, the way he kissed my head and arms and legs.

Then he held me until he fell asleep.

I felt the warmth of his body, the softness of his breathing as he slept. I wondered what would have happened if we had stayed together. Could we have gotten to this place while we were still married, or would we have continued our anger and fear as long as we were both there as daily reminders of it? Did we need to live our own lives for a while so we could find joy in each other again?

Why had we missed all those years together? Because of anger and blame—letting them get the better of love.

Death is not the thief of time. Guilt is.

DAY NINETEEN

I woke up next to Joe in the middle of the night, and I felt the greatest joy and greatest sadness I've experienced in a long time. I lay in bed for a minute before I got up to use the bathroom, listening to the sound of his breathing. Rhythmic and steady.

When I came back to bed, he rolled over, half awake, and gathered me in his arms as if receiving me. "Are you okay?" he asked.

"I am," I said. I rested my head on his chest, tucked my feet between his legs, and felt completely at home.

Joe drifted back to sleep instantly, but I lay awake for a few minutes. I heard Daddy's clock strike two a.m., the soft swishing of the ceiling fan above us, the hum of the air-conditioning as it cycled on and off. Each sound so ordinary, so remarkable, like a small symphony in the hush of the night.

So this is what it means to be alive, I thought.

Maybe what led me to take the pearls wasn't despair. Maybe it was numbness and resignation. I don't know that I turned away from life. I think I simply forgot what it is.

I've debated whether to tell him about the pearls, just

as I did with Father David. I think it would make him feel guilty, and now that I know the liberation of guiltlessness, I want the same for him.

And yet, if there's a chance for us to have a real partnership again, it can't be built on secrets.

Joe said he saw the cats this morning. He got up early and had the coffee going before I got out of bed.

"I put out some food for them," he said, "and all of them came right away."

He filled a mug with coffee and handed it to me.

"What do you mean, all of them?" I said.

"The mother cat and the four kittens," he said.

"They were all here?"

I looked out the door at the porch. Sure enough, one kitten crouched at the food bowl, eating. One sat on a chair, grooming itself. And the other two chased each other out in the yard while the mama cat watched, unconcerned. Just as if it happened this way every day.

"Yep," he said. "You called them here. It worked."

I felt relief wash through me, but right behind it came the wave of sadness I'd felt in the middle of the night.

Once again, I thought, *I gave up too soon.*

Responding to an inner prompting last night, I pulled a pound of bacon from the freezer and defrosted it. I made Joe a real breakfast, just like I did when we were first married.

The crackle of the bacon frying sounded so crisp and clear, it filled the entire house. When I poured milk into the eggs and whisked them together, it reminded me of stirring the paint in those old cans until the colors came to life. I sank deeper into the sensations, feeling the power of brushing paint on the wall without any limitations.

I remembered running through the backyard with Holly

when we were girls. Jumping off the couch and dancing through the living room.

My body remembered the feel of Rose's hair when I braided it for school. The cool water of the lake the night Joe proposed. The force of the wind the day we were married.

The smell of the breakfast almost overwhelmed me—not in the nauseous kind of way I experienced during my pregnancy with Rose, but with a sweet sensation that brought me to a halt.

I stood by the kitchen table, one hand on the smooth back of the chair, and closed my eyes, breathing in the aroma as though awakening from a long sleep.

I remembered when I was little, before Daddy's accident, when Mama made these kinds of breakfasts. It made me think of September days, when the morning air was cool, the sky overcast and threatening rain, while the house was lit up like a star, and the swaddling smell enticed me out of bed, wrapping me in a blanket of comfort.

It will be September in a few days. I don't know if I'll ever have that experience of a September morning again. But I have the memory now. And for now, that's more than enough.

All these years, I could have been remembering hundreds of beautiful moments with Rose and Mama. And I chose to lose my heart to sadness instead. I would do it differently now. For whatever time I have left, I will remember the joy, not the heartache.

"Joe," I said as I set the platter of bacon on the table, "how about if we go visit Rose today?"

This afternoon, we stopped at Nancy's to pick up some flowers.

She squealed when she saw the two of us together. She came out from behind the counter, wiped her hands on her pants, and gave both of us a big hug.

"Good lord, Joe," she said, "this is the best surprise. Where did you come from?"

"I think Meg conjured me up," he said, giving me the same look he did when we were dating.

"Heavens, girl, you look good," Nancy said. "I've missed you, but it looks like you've been getting lots of rest."

"Too much," I said. I'd put on my blue sundress, which makes my hair look almost as red as it did in high school. My long nights of sleep have erased the circles under my eyes, and my skin is tan from all the time I've spent in the yard the last couple of weeks, trying to restore balance to the plants.

"Thank you for giving me the time off," I said. "I didn't realize how much I needed it." Without thinking, I pulled a couple of spent blooms from a pink petunia on the counter.

"You're sure welcome," Nancy said. "Really, you've been doing me a big favor."

She kept looking back and forth between the two of us, as though she couldn't believe what she was seeing.

She turned back to the cash register, put a stack of twenties in the drawer, and closed it with a snap. "Business has been so slow, you know. But it'll pick up. I hear there's finally some rain in the forecast."

She leaned on the counter and stared at us. "I have to tell you how happy it makes me to see my two favorite people together. Right as rain, that's what it is."

"I agree," Joe said. "We're on our way to the cemetery and wanted to pick up some flowers."

"Sure, sure," she said, "just pick out whatever you want." She chatted with Joe while I gathered flowers from the coolers and wrapped them in tissue paper, taking in every detail, every scent and color, just in case it was the last time.

* * *

On a Saturday afternoon a couple of weeks before Rose was born, Joe told me he was running up to Mama's to fix her kitchen faucet.

"Shouldn't take long," he said. I was stretched out on the sofa in the family room, reading *Better Homes and Gardens* and moving as little as possible. My enormous middle had taken charge of my body, and I could do little but obey it. My doctor never said I needed bed rest, but my ankles did.

"Need anything before I go?" he said.

I looked around at the stash of magazines, the glass of water, the bag of carrots, and the TV remote, all within reach.

"Nope, I think I'm set," I said.

"Okay," he said, kissing me good-bye. "See you in an hour or so."

I lay back and looked out the window at the burning bush in the yard. It had turned bright red, so much so that in late afternoon, it cast a pink glow inside the house. It pleased me to know that one of the first things Rose would see in this new life of hers was a shrub at the height of its fall color.

After a few minutes, I got up to go to the bathroom for the twentieth time that day. It was not an easy task to heave myself off the couch or lower myself onto the toilet, but I managed, feeling elephantine and catching a glimpse of my swollen face in the bathroom mirror.

Then, panic.

We were almost out of toilet paper.

I'd been going through it at the speed of light, and I hadn't been keeping up on household inventory since I'd spent so much time lazing around.

I used the last bits of paper on the roll, then waddled to the kitchen to call Mama. I figured Joe could run to Ted's Market and get some on his way home.

"How's the faucet coming along?" I asked Mama when she picked up the phone.

She paused. "Faucet?"

"Yeah, the one Joe's fixing."

Another pause. "Hmmm. I'm not sure what you're talking about."

I lowered myself into a kitchen chair, puzzled.

"He left here about thirty minutes ago," I said. "He told me he was headed to your place to fix your leaky faucet."

"Well," she said, "it's news to me. Maybe the faucet belongs to someone else and he just said my name by mistake."

"Maybe," I said, knowing Joe didn't get confused very often.

"Is there something you need?" Mama asked, hearing the perplexed tone in my voice.

"No," I said, "just toilet paper. For some reason it disappears faster than usual when you pee seventy times a day." I tried to keep it light.

"That's not too big a crisis, then," she said. "Sounds like Joe can take care of it when he gets back. Or do you want me to run some down to your place to tide you over?"

"That's okay," I said. "I think I'm good for a while. Thanks."

"Well, you know I'm always here if you need anything," she said.

"I know, Mama. Love you."

"Love you, too."

I wish I could say that I stayed calm, that my hormonal mind didn't conjure up every worst possible scenario. But within five minutes, I'd decided that Joe was having an affair, probably with the new geologist who had interned in his office the previous summer. That was why he'd been "working overtime."

He couldn't stand my girth and my sloth-like manner. He'd had enough of walking me to the bathroom in the middle of the night, and doing all the vacuuming and dusting. And who could blame him, really, when we couldn't do any of the things we used to enjoy together? When he'd soon be saddled with a wife who might never shrink to her former size and a child who would depend on him to keep her safe?

I envisioned myself as a single mother. I wondered how we'd negotiate visitation, especially if he married his mistress. How would I go on without him? How would I keep from ripping both of them apart with my bare hands?

And then I heard a car in the driveway. I dabbed at my eyes with a wad of tissue and tried to dislodge myself from the couch.

When Joe walked in, he was beaming until he saw my face. "What's wrong?" he said, immediately concerned. "Are you okay? Is the baby okay?"

"We're okay," I said, blubbering like a five-year-old. "But where have you been? And be honest with me. I know you weren't at Mama's."

"Uh-oh," he said, his voice soothing. He gathered me up in his arms to console me. "Come on," he said. "I'll show you what I was up to."

He took me by the hand and led me to the side door and out onto the stoop.

"What do you think?" he said.

There in the driveway sat a brand-new SUV.

"Joe, what did you do?" I said, overjoyed and confused. All thoughts of a mistress melted away. I wouldn't have to raise Rose alone. And we wouldn't be carting our baby around in our old clunker.

"I've been saving up to surprise you," he said.

"You mean you've been keeping secrets from me?" I

teased, now happy that he had. He helped me down the steps and over to the driveway, where I ran my hands over the beige hood as though I were petting a cat.

"Yep," he said, opening the driver's door and adjusting the seat to accommodate my enormous middle. "I had a reason for all that overtime I've been putting in."

Before I tried to climb in, I looked in the backseat, and what I saw was even better than the vehicle itself: our infant car seat, the one Holly gave me at my baby shower. Joe had tied pink ribbons all over it. We'd been so afraid of losing this baby after all the miscarriages, we'd hardly dared to hope that this pregnancy would take.

Those ribbons made it real, as though Joe acknowledged that it was going to happen, and that made it okay for me to rejoice in our child, too. Looking up at him from that driver's seat, I could see it in his eyes, as though we both exhaled for the first time in months.

He never gave me reason to doubt him. Never.

We went to the cemetery with flowers for Rose, Mama, and Daddy. Two days ago, I would have dreaded it. Today, I felt nothing but peace. The peace which passeth understanding. We walked through the cemetery arm in arm, and I felt I could gently lift off the ground and go perch in a tree like the robins and goldfinches flying around us.

I've always hated cemeteries. The gray stones, the somber symmetry. The ache of sorrow and memory that lingers there. But today I sensed something much different.

"Do you feel it?" I asked Joe when we sat down on a bench near Rose.

"What's that, Meg?" he said.

"The joy," I said, realizing I couldn't explain it if he asked me.

He didn't seem startled. "Yes," he said. "I think I do."

The flowering bushes growing in the cemetery look tired

but regal. I could see every cut in the tombstones. The beauty of all the lives represented by those markers. The serene order of the military section—now like my house. Everything in place.

Life has become so rich and full and endless. That's the irony. It has become endless in the end.

Death is not an end, it is a beginning—it's true. And when you live without fear of it, there is no shortage of moments. That's the ultimate mystery. I have tomorrow, or maybe thirty more years. I can practically count the minutes to the time Sunday night when it will be exactly twenty days since I took the pearls.

Yet I feel like moments are endless now, that each one of them contains a vast universe of potential. Like the stamen of a flower. Everything it's connected to is eternal, and the drops of pollen it produces are infinite, too.

I see infinity in a flower and realize that I don't need to regret my decision or worry or fear or judge it. Because I have changed nothing that matters, and I have changed everything that matters.

I was right that this isn't a regular suicide. In fact, I can hardly bring myself to use that word. I said from the beginning that I simply accelerated the end of my cycle, the same way the drought has accelerated it for my flowers this summer. Yet my situation also is not like someone who receives a cancer diagnosis and has only a few weeks to live.

I'm experiencing something in between—a death by my own hands, yet one that allows me to learn all the lessons of living I missed in the past fifty-five years. Like all the kids I worked with at the hospital, like Rose and my mom, I get to experience the end as the beginning, and to look at life without fear before I let it go.

Why didn't I know this? Why didn't I realize that any day could be the beginning rather than the end?

We sat on a bench in the rose garden at the cemetery,

looking out over the neat rows of stones, recognizing names I'd grown up with, and that Joe had come to know. That's when Joe asked me about looking ahead, about being together.

"We used to know how to make each other happy," he said. "I think we could remember how to do that."

I took a deep breath. "I'm not sure," I said. My words were as much about my decision to share my secret as they were about our future.

"Meg, don't let death stand in the way of life."

"It may be too late," I said.

"No," he said, touching my cheek. "We could start over."

"You don't understand," I said as I felt the struggle within my mind. Maybe that was the problem all along. I'd tried to figure out what was right rather than trusting my heart.

As I felt Joe close beside me and looked out over the names of my family, I felt a surge inside me, as though a door in my heart opened.

And so I told him the truth. All of it. My loneliness, the anger, the feeling of being done with life. I told him what it was like after he left and I couldn't breathe anymore. I told him how Mama saved me by needing my care, and how I watched her disappear bit by bit, knowing I couldn't do a thing to stop it.

I told him how empty the house was when I came home every day. How I sometimes looked out over the hills and saw the ghosts of everyone I've lost.

I told him about opening the freezer door and reaching to the back for the small bottle of pearls. About twisting off the lid and stirring the contents into my yogurt until they melted as though they'd never existed at all.

I told him about Dr. Edelman's peaceful passing and about my lab tests, as clean as the day I was born. About the regret and the anticipation, side by side. And I told him the one thing I know for sure: that today I would make a different decision. And yet I'm no longer angry. No longer lonely.

And then I said the two words I needed to say not just to him but also to myself.

"I'm sorry."

He sat silent through the whole thing, staring off into the sky. I didn't know what he would do, but I was certain he wouldn't push me away.

When I was done, he asked one thing: "Are you sure it can't be reversed?"

"I'm sure," I said. "But I don't know what will happen. Maybe nothing will happen. Maybe we'll be sitting on the porch together night after night for the rest of our lives."

Joe turned to look at me, and I saw tears running down both of his cheeks.

"That's why it's important every day to let you know that I love you," I said, stroking his face. "Always have. Always will."

DAY TWENTY

It's cool outside. Joe is asleep in the bedroom. I can hear his soft snores as I write. It's 10:57 p.m. Daddy's clock will strike eleven in three minutes, and I'll have just under five hours to go.

I have no idea what will happen between now and daybreak, so all I can do is write. I feel that I need to say something profound. Do I wish I could be around to live this life with Joe? Yes, and yet it's not so simple.

This is new for me, to look at death not as an ending but as a sign of continuity. In a way, Daddy's passing served as a bridge to my life with Joe. Even though I couldn't see it at the time, Rose's death and Mama's opened doors as surely as they closed them. We are all connecting links. And sometimes when we step out of the chain, we allow new connections that could not have happened with us there.

I'm ready. That's a big statement, I know. I don't even know what I'm ready for. If I die, I feel sure that Rose and Mama and Daddy will be there to meet me. And if I don't, I'm ready for whatever life looks like after today.

I've never said that before. I've always thought I had to have the answers, to control what life looks like. For the first time, I'm willing to live today and not know what will happen after this.

Joe and I spent the day together. Again, he had the coffee ready when I got up, and we sat nestled together in silence on the porch while the morning still felt cool. No blame. No judgment. No trying to fix something that can't be changed. Just the deep comfort of acceptance.

The trees are turning, partly from the drought, but also from the approach of fall. There's a hint of red in the burning bush, and the leaves on the lindens are prematurely golden. I sat on the swing with Joe, his arm around me, and looked out at the hills where I've walked my whole life.

This may *be* my whole life. It may end today. I haven't seen any more moles disappear, there are no other signs that the pearls are working, or that the shutoff moment is going to happen.

We did a little bit of nothing today. He finished patching and painting the ceiling in the bathroom, fixing it so completely that you'd never know there had been damage.

I picked a bouquet from the memorial garden and put the flowers in one of Mama's vases. Long stems of hosta blooms and fronds from the painted ferns—the perfect combination of strength and softness.

I laughed every time Joe opened a cupboard or a drawer because he gave me the strangest look. "I thought I was the organized one," he said when he opened the bathroom closet.

All the towels were stacked neatly and grouped by color. I put all the unopened toiletries in one handsome basket and threw away the old cough syrups and half-used jars of Vaseline. One shelf had just my hair dryer and a package of toilet paper—nothing else.

It's that way everywhere in this house. All those clothes

and boxes that were half hidden or covered in cobwebs are gone. Receipts and paid bills sit in an accordion file in Mama's desk rather than spilling out of a drawer, and all the old paperwork has been shredded, returning to the earth as mulch in the flower beds.

The whole place feels lighter and stronger at the same time.

Over lunch, I pulled out an album with photos of Rose, and we looked at it together. All her first-day-of-school pictures. The photo of her with Brent and Mark after Mama taught them how to make fake teeth from watermelon rinds. A picture of her saddled up on Romeo for the very first time, looking perfectly at ease.

"We were lucky to have her," Joe said.

"We were," I agreed. "Even for a little while."

She'd be twenty-six now. I think about what she'd look like, what her voice would sound like. Maybe if Joe and I had taken it one day at a time after Rose died, rather than looking back and looking forward, we would have stayed together.

Maybe losing a child isn't the worst thing that can happen to you. Maybe the worst thing that can happen is to not live the life you're given, to let guilt and anger steal your life from you.

I tried not to read double meaning into everything we did and said today, but I couldn't help it. Everything mattered.

This afternoon we played gin rummy and each won a game. "Two out of three?" Joe asked, waving the cards in front of me.

"I think I'm good," I said. "I like calling it even."

We joked that, after such strenuous card games, we deserved ice cream sundaes, so we got out two of the biggest cereal bowls in the cupboard, filled them with butter brickle ice cream, and piled on chocolate chips and nuts.

And later in the afternoon, when I called Holly just to say hello, I told her I had a surprise, then handed the phone to Joe.

"Hey, Holly," he said, winking at me.

"Joe? What are *you* doing there?" I could hear the joy in her voice all the way across the room.

When I got back on the phone with her, she nearly burst into tears.

"This is one of the best days of my life," she said.

"Mine, too," I told her.

Joe and I decided to have a date at home tonight, so I changed into my new dress. I gathered up my hair the way Miriam had during the power outage, and I put on lipstick and a touch of mascara.

When I reached into the bathroom closet for a towel, I pulled out the white tufted one—the one that made me realize how my vision has changed. I felt the luxuriousness of it all over again, running my hand over the texture and seeing the beauty in its folds.

I'm seeing everything with those new eyes now, including myself.

When I walked into the living room, Joe looked up from the couch and whistled.

"You look beautiful," he said, "just like the day I met you."

He cued up some music, took me in his arms, and we danced in the living room, swaying in rhythm with each other. It felt as familiar as putting on a comfortable pair of shoes.

"You always were a good dancer," I said.

He kissed me lightly on top of the head.

And then I saw them. The colored lights, swirling all around me.

"They're here," I said to Joe, and he held me closer.

He's the only living person I could say that to and know he understands what I mean.

"Can I tell you a secret?" I asked Joe over dinner.

"Another?" he said, reaching across the table and taking my hand. "At this point, I think you can tell me anything."

I'd given it a lot of thought, and I wanted to share something with him that I'd never told anyone—not even Mama, who, toward the end, seemed like my priest. I'd tell her things in confession because I knew she wouldn't remember.

One day when she stretched out on the sofa under the crocheted afghan, I sat down to rub her feet, which prompted a memory.

"I used to go down to the creek by myself when I was little," I told her, "even when you warned me about the danger. One day I fell in the water and got my tennis shoes covered with mud, so I rinsed them off and set them in the sun to dry. I hid the evidence and made sure my shoes didn't squeak when I came home."

She peered at me sideways, and I thought maybe this time she was upset by my disobedience, even if it had happened forty years earlier.

"Don't you think it's time for a haircut?" she said.

Like I said, complete confidentiality.

I confessed to smoking a couple of cigarettes when I was fifteen and babysitting Miriam. I confessed to having sex with Joe in the shed while we were dating, while Mama fixed pork chops for us in the kitchen. I confessed to wishing Mama would marry the man who owned the variety store because he smelled good and I figured he probably had money, and I thought he might make her happy.

But I never told her about the joy I felt when Rose died.

Tonight, it felt right to share that with Joe.

"Remember the moment when we were both in the hospital room with Rose," I said, "the moment when we knew she was gone?"

"Yes," he said quietly.

"Before the grief hit me," I said, "I felt a jubilation."

I told him how, just for a moment, I wanted to shout, "We did it!" He and Rose and I created a trinity that sailed her through this life and into the next as clearly as a boat crossing in the light of the moon. For just an instant, and totally without warning, my soul celebrated our triumph.

Maybe I felt the joy of the other side, I told him. But immediately after, the full impact of the grief rolled over me like a freight train and turned the joy to guilt. What was wrong with me? How could a mother feel joy at the loss of her child?

Joe listened quietly and took it all in.

"I can see everything more clearly now," I said. "I wasn't celebrating the loss, but the feeling that we expressed the fullest love we could while we had Rose with us."

He squeezed my hand, tears in his eyes.

"Now," I said, "I can see that the joy, just like the sadness, has been with me all along."

Will I wake up tomorrow morning? I don't know. The colored swirls didn't take me by surprise, but they didn't answer any questions, either. Are they here because they're welcoming me into the next world, or because my vision has opened up, the way it did when I was little?

Maybe I've already awoken. Because I know, in a way I didn't just three weeks ago, that this life is precious and beautiful and mysterious and wondrous even in its pain. I have spent so much of my life asleep, and now, just at the point where it might end, I see it as though it's all new.

The thought of going makes me almost burst with longing for what I'll leave behind. How could I have missed so much beauty and all the miracles along the way? How could there be an ending to forgiveness and love?

This is a world without end. And I know now, in a way I've never known before, that I am forever alive.

Ironically, it's starting to mist outside. I pulled a sweater from my closet to put around my shoulders as I sit on the porch and smell the sweet scent of rain.

It's been so long since we've had any here that it's like seeing a spaceship flying overhead and dropping little gray men to the ground. It is that remarkable and new.

But then again, everything feels that way to me now. I have been renewed by the touch of my husband's hand, by the gentleness of Father David, by the innocence of my nephews and niece, the love of my sister, even by the care of a Chinese healer half a continent away.

I wonder if this is why we're in relationships. To remember who we are. To know the love within us rather than the bitterness.

It seems odd that I'm not scared now. I've seen so many people live their whole lives afraid of dying. All I can do is forgive myself for making this decision.

It seems to me that the most important thing is to forgive.

I used to think that forgiveness meant letting someone off the hook, denying that their betrayal hurt my soul. But now I can see forgiveness in a whole new light. I need to forgive myself for expecting this world, my life, to be different from how it is, to arrange itself according to my expectations.

I let the world be as it is. I accept my decision, my life, my death, whenever it comes.

I suppose that's why I sit here under the stars tonight, listening to the sound of Joe breathing through the open window, feeling the breeze, smelling the rich smell of the productive soil. And I remember the love, not the sadness or the loss.

I'm so happy to leave the plants with rain. I spent some time alone with them today, talking to them, cupping their blooms in my hands. I don't know if it's the promise of rain or the powder from Lin Chow that I fed them a few days ago, but they look fresh and rejuvenated. They're ready for what's next, like me.

I'm going to go inside, slip into bed beside Joe, and let the sound of rain carry me into sleep. I have to admit that there's a deep sadness inside. But when I think about seeing Daddy and Rose and Mama before the night is through, I feel like I'm holding on to something so deep and everlasting that sadness and fear have no power at all.

Most of all, there is indescribable joy to know this: I may wake up tomorrow morning with Joe handing me a cup of coffee and saying, "Didn't want you to miss this sunrise."

Or before that sun rises, I may be reunited with the three people I have missed the most.

I don't know what will happen as I sleep tonight, or where I'll awaken. But I do know one thing for sure. Either way I'll be in heaven, looking straight into the eyes of love.

Lillian's Coconut Cake

2 c. sugar
1 stick butter, softened
½ c. shortening
1 tsp. vanilla
5 eggs, separated
2 c. flour
1 tsp. baking soda
½ tsp. salt
1 c. buttermilk
1 ⅓ c. sweetened shredded coconut

Cream sugar, butter, shortening, and vanilla. Add egg yolks and beat until combined. Add flour, baking soda, and salt, alternating with buttermilk. Stir in coconut. Beat egg whites until stiff peaks form, then carefully fold into the batter.

Grease and flour three 9-inch cake pans, then line the bottoms with waxed paper and grease again. Spread batter equally in the pans and bake at 350 degrees for about 20 to 25 minutes, until a toothpick inserted in the center comes out clean.

Cool on racks for 10 minutes, then carefully remove the cake layers from pans and let cool completely.

Frosting

1 stick butter, softened
1 8-ounce package cream cheese
1 box powdered sugar
1 tsp. vanilla
½ c. sweetened flaked coconut

Cream butter and cream cheese. Add powdered sugar and vanilla and beat until creamy and spreadable. Frost cake and sprinkle coconut over the top.

TWENTY

Debra Landwehr Engle

ABOUT THIS GUIDE

The following questions are intended to
enhance your group's reading of
Twenty.

DISCUSSION QUESTIONS

1. At the beginning of the story, Meg feels overwhelmed by loss, grief, and a lack of purpose as she looks at the years ahead. She appears only partially committed to ending her life, yet she takes the pearls anyway. Why do you think she makes this decision when she's not sure what she wants or what the outcome will be?

2. Meg says that her action isn't a regular suicide. Do you agree or disagree? What makes it different? Does the twenty-day window change the definition of her decision?

3. In the story, the weather plays an important role, as the drought mirrors how parched Meg feels inside. It also makes her feel more helpless and despondent. How much are you influenced by your environment? What do you do to feel better when you're dealing with extreme conditions in your external life?

4. While the green pearls are fictional, many people believe that terminally ill patients should have the right to assisted suicide. When Dr. Edelman gives Meg the pearls, he says, "[S]ometimes helping people cross that threshold from pain to peace is the greatest gift you can give them." Do you agree or disagree?

5. Meg finds purpose in tying up loose ends, even though she doesn't know if she's preparing for life or death. What if we lived our lives as though we didn't have much time left? Is there value in this?

6. What are some of the things Meg does that you would also do in her situation? For instance, cleaning? Visiting family? Giving things away? Reconnecting? What would you do differently?

7. Meg's housecleaning mirrors the ways she's clearing out her inner life. If you were to get rid of one thing that takes up space in your heart and mind, what would it be? For instance, guilt? Shame? Worry? Judgment? Doubt?

8. What events in the story give Meg hope? What role does hope play in our lives?

9. As Joe comes back into Meg's life, she learns many lessons about love and the cost of keeping it at arm's length. Why do we sometimes cut ourselves off from love? Which of Meg's lessons resonate most with you?

10. Why is forgiveness so essential for Meg to finally heal from her past? What role has forgiveness played in your life?

11. Meg eventually sees every moment of life as a gift. Have you had such a moment? If so, what was it like? How did it change your perspective on the challenges life often brings?

12. What does Meg mean at the end when she says, "Either way I'll be in heaven, looking straight into the eyes of love"? What do you think happens to Meg in the end? Why?

Connect with U s

Visit us online at
KensingtonBooks.com
to read more from your favorite authors, see books
by series, view reading group guides, and more.

for sneak peeks, chances to win books and prize packs,
and to share your thoughts with other readers.

facebook.com/kensingtonpublishing
twitter.com/kensingtonbooks

Tell us what you think!
To share your thoughts, submit a review,
or sign up for our eNewsletters, please visit:
KensingtonBooks.com/TellUs.